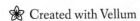

LEIA STONE

TRIGGER WARNING

Violence and battle scenes are present in this book.

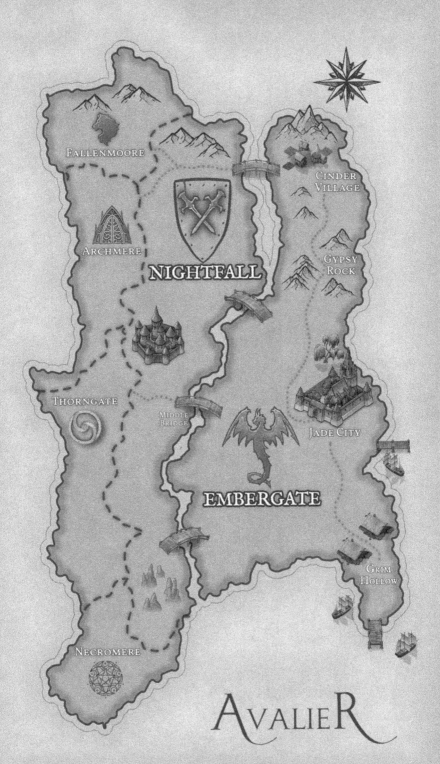

"You don't have to do this," my elder brother Cyrus said as he paced the floor of the home I shared with my younger brother Oslo. Our parents were long gone, and now it was just me and my two brothers. Cyrus was married off with two pups of his own and little Oslo lived with me.

I looked up at him. "Yes I do. It's mandatory, Cy; the summons says that the most dominant female—"

Cyrus cut me off, looming over me with his towering height. "I don't care about the summons! The king will have plenty of wives to choose from, no need to get killed trying to—"

"Excuse me?" I stood on my tiptoes and poked him in the chest; now it was my turn to cut him off. "You don't think I can win?"

Cyrus looked slightly ashamed. "Zara, I trained you myself, I know you are a powerful warrior, but to go against *all* of the most dominant females in Fallenmoore just to win the king's hand?"

Silence descended on the room. I didn't want this opportunity, especially not with Axil Moon. We had a history, one that I tried to forget every summer. Cyrus knew that. But we had received a mandatory order and I was no coward.

"To enter the Queen Trials means death," my little brother said from his spot on the couch, looking up at me like a scared little boy. At twelve years old he could fend for himself if I died, but I was like a mother figure to him. He'd have no one to tuck him in at night or show him the ways of the wolf.

"What about the status this would bring to our family?" I asked them. "The positions of power you and Oslo would get if I won?"

My brothers were dominant – but not dominant enough to be alpha of our pack, and yet not submissive enough to be taken care of by its members either. They fought over resources and had to fend for themselves, like most midpack wolves. If I entered the trials and won, not only would I become queen of our people, but it would also launch both of my brothers into a place where they were paid dues simply for breathing. The family of the queen wanted for nothing. New furs every winter, food and lodging that was all gifted by the king, and they were given places of honor in the royal wolven army.

My elder brother crossed his arms and assessed me with his gaze. I was twenty summers old now; he could not deny that I had grown into a woman. I could hold the stare of even the strongest male members of my pack without cowering and my muscles looked like they'd been carved from stone. I was no longer the little scrappy girl he'd taught to fight by the riverbank. I was third in command of this pack, just under the alpha and his second. That was no small feat for a female.

"Zara, if you win, you would have to marry King Axil. You're okay with that? After your history together?" he asked.

"What history?" my little brother piped up

"You don't need to know," Cyrus and I both shot back.

I swore I could still feel Axil's lips on mine when I closed my eyes at night and thought about those two summer months at the dominant wolves training camp when we were fifteen.

My first love. Or what I'd thought was love when I was just a little pup. I was basically a mother to my little brother even then, constantly weighed down with the responsibilities of household duties. Axil had been a breath of fresh air. I hadn't known he was the prince at the time; I lived in a tiny village far from Death Mountain, where the royal court resided. We'd laughed and talked for hours. Kissed under the moonlight and danced until our feet felt like they were going to fall off. For two months straight I ate, drank, and breathed Axil Moon. It was only when his elder brother caught us making out that last day of camp that I realized who he was, and everything came crashing to a halt.

I could still remember the fight they'd had right in front of me.

"I love her," Axil had told his brother.

"You don't love women like that, Axil, you bed them and move on to someone more suitable from Death Mountain. You're a prince, start acting like one. Let's go, before someone sees you."

I'd been crushed. Axil had spoken of a future together, of wanting to visit me and me him, of one day wanting to marry me. I'd expected him to tell his brother to eat dirt but instead he'd lowered his head and walked away without another word.

He just left. Throwing me away like villager trash. It's not like I had any idea he was Prince Axil, brother of King Ansel, or that I'd just had a fling with royalty that would never happen again. I was beneath him.

"Zara." Cyrus brought me back to the moment.

I looked my brother in the eyes, holding his gaze easily. "Yes, I would marry him. To prove that a villager from the Mud Flats can make a queen," I snarled, a growl building deep in my throat. And to prove to Axil

Moon *and* his brother that I was good enough. Status did not make a queen in Fallenmoore. Brute force, dominance, cunning, and power in battle did. The trials were a literal fight to the death – or forfeit, but no one with any self-respect did that. You would be torn apart by your pack and bring your family shame for three generations.

My brother appraised me differently now, walking around me in a slow circle. "That's the attitude you would need to win this."

We were back in our roles of coach and student. I'd been sparring with Cyrus since I was three years old and barely learning to shift into my wolf form.

"Dorian would be sad to lose you. You will need his permission." My brother spoke of our alpha. Cyrus was right. As the most dominant female member of our pack I would be a loss to the Mud Flat pack. I kept all of the other dominant women in line but if I did this, if I won the trials, I would bring great honor to Dorian and all of my packmates. I was still holding my brother's gaze, waiting for his approval. In our weird little family, he was like a father to me and I wouldn't enter without his okay.

The summons came in as a mandatory invitation, but if the alpha of the pack didn't want to let that specific female go, or she was already spoken for romantically, another could be sent in her stead. Morgan could go in my place; she was the next in line of succession where dominance was concerned.

"Go ask him. If he says yes, I'll train you," my brother finally said, breaking eye contact with me.

Cyrus was a well-sought-after battle trainer. He might not have been dominant enough to be an alpha, but his cunning and strategy in fights was unmatched in our area. He'd even traveled to Death Mountain to train some of the Royal Guard. What he lacked in muscle he made up for in intelligence.

"I'll tell him. Not ask." I corrected my brother's submissive thinking.

Cyrus chuckled. "Good luck with that."

Dorian was a fair alpha, tough at times, but fair. The term "tough love" must have been coined for him. When I was thirteen, I stole some extra food from the community storeroom because I was bored and he starved me for four days and nights with water only. I never stole food again. Dorian earned respect; he didn't ask for it blindly.

Nodding to my brother, I grasped the summons that had come from Death Mountain. It had gone out to all cities and villages in Fallenmoore and this one had my name on it. I wondered if Axil even knew that I'd be coming or if his advisors had sent this to me. It had been five years since I saw him, a boy who was now king.

I swooped down to ruffle my little brother's hair.

"Be right back."

Oslo seemed sad, and I knew he didn't want this for me because it could take me away from him. Bending down, I looked him right in the eyes, holding his gaze. "If I become queen, you can come live with me at Death Mountain palace," I told him, and his entire face lit up.

"Really?"

I nodded and he glanced away, no longer able to look into my eyes. He was the most submissive in our family and it made me want to protect him all the more.

"What if you die?" he asked, his voice small.

Cyrus reached out and roughed him up a bit, shaking his shoulders tightly and forcing Oslo to punch him to get him off. "Then she dies with honor and we will howl her name at the moon every year in remembrance," Cyrus said.

Cyrus was right, dying during the Queen Trials was a great honor.

The contest to become queen only happened when the king needed a wife. My mother traveled to the city and saw the trials with Axil's father, and three years ago I'd followed the one with his brother Ansel closely from here, but I never got to go see it in person. Axil took the pack from his brother the following year in a challenge fight, leaving him alive as a mercy.

Stepping out of my home, I made my way across the village square. The pack was out and about. Some of the women were skinning a fresh kill and a few men were in wolf form, sparring off to the side and practicing their hunting takedowns. A fresh hut was being built for a newly married couple and the sun was high in the sky. It was a beautiful day in our sleepy village but I knew if I did this, I would be yanked from my normal and into the bustling capital city of Death Mountain.

I knocked on the door of Dorian's home and he called out immediately. "Come in, Zara."

I grinned: damn, his sense of smell was second to none. I opened the door and found him eating a plate of meat and potatoes. His wife was tending a pot on the stove and nodded to me as I walked in.

Amara was the most submissive member of our pack. She rarely ever made eye contact and avoided confrontation at all costs. She was a peacemaker, which I loved about her. Any civil dispute was brought to Amara first to see if there was a more harmonious outcome possible. If that wasn't the case, it was brought to me and I was the harsher problem solver. They called me "the punisher" because I liked to dole out penalties like those that Dorian had given to me, in order to teach wolves lessons they would never forget. Until you had felt the pangs of hunger eating your stomach inside and out, you didn't know what it was like to want to *really* want to steal food, and you'd never do it out of boredom. It toughened me and taught me things I felt would serve me better than a slap on the wrist.

I pulled up a chair, dropped the summons in front of my alpha and then sat down.

"I got one too," he said, sucking on a piece of meat and then he looked up at me and I held Dorian's gaze. My alpha was nearly as big as a bearin. He was packed with muscle and though he was over forty winters old, he moved with the speed and grace of a trained killer. His short-cropped hair was dark brown, threaded through with gray that bled into his salt-and-pepper beard. But it was his eyes that held me now, deep brown with flecks of yellow; they felt like they pierced my very soul when I looked into them.

Dorian and I sat there for a full minute just staring at each other while Amara whistled to herself and stirred whatever was in the pot on the stove. It felt like a heavy weight had settled over my shoulders while my mind wanted me to look away, but my willpower was much stronger. Just when I thought I might go insane holding that stare, he spoke.

"You really want to do this?" he asked and I broke his gaze to look down at the summons, catching my breath after the sustained eye contact. I had to show him I was capable of this, that I was strong enough to do it.

"I do. I want to bring honor to our people and show the fancy king and his brother that a girl from Mud Flat pack can wipe the floor with any of his city wolves."

My alpha grinned but then his smile faltered. "And competing for Axil Moon's heart is okay with you?"

My breath hitched. Dorian had been the one to pick me up from camp that summer. After Axil had broken me, Dorian, Amara and Cyrus had been the ones to help put me back together. He knew how badly Axil's rejection had affected me.

I met his stare, trying to hide the vulnerability I was feeling. "I have to. I need to show Axil Moon that he was wrong about me."

Dorian nodded curtly. "Then I have one condition, Zara."

"Name it." I sat erect.

"My condition is that you do not forfeit," he stated. "I want you to be queen or to die trying."

Chills rushed down my spine and I swallowed hard. Of course I wanted that too. I'd always been taught it was dishonorable to tap out, but ... if it really came down to it, could I just ... allow myself to be killed to keep honor in my pack?

I had the distinct feeling this was another one of his lessons. To see how badly I wanted this, how ready I was for it.

He leaned forward, his eyes suddenly gleaming with emotion. "Zara, you have always been my favorite. But if you bend the knee to some pompous city wolf, I will have to kill you myself and I don't want to do that."

Amara stopped stirring and made a whining sound in her throat. But Dorian's words gave me pride, there was a compliment layered deep somewhere in there.

"I will win or I will die trying, Alpha," I promised him.

He reached for the paper and handed me back the summons. "Then reply yes. I assume Cyrus is training you?"

I nodded. "Yes, Alpha."

"You only have two weeks to prepare. I'll help train you as well. And Morgan will join us."

My heart pinched with pride. For the alpha to take time away from all the busy dealings of running a pack of over fifty wolves was a big deal.

"Thank you, Alpha. I'll make you proud," I vowed and stood, grasping the summons tightly between my fingers.

He gave me a curt nod and then went back to tearing into his elkin meat. As I turned to leave, Amara streaked across the room and pulled me into a hug.

I was caught off guard at first. Dominant wolves weren't big on displays of emotion so I wasn't keen on hugging, but Amara was like a second mother to me. When my own mother died in childbirth with Oslo, I was only eight years old. My father, the last alpha of our pack, before Dorian, had died a few months prior in a bearin attack on a hunting trip. Our entire family was devastated with the loss of our mom and dad.

But the pack had rallied around us, to help make sure we had what we needed until we came of age and could fend for ourselves. They brought food, blankets, came to clean the house and play with us. But it was Amara, who was in her early twenties at the time, newly married to the alpha, who had come every single night for four years and sung me and Oslo to sleep. She would pat our backs and sing old songs that my mother used to when I was a young babe. She taught me how to feed Oslo from a milk bag and to change his soiled linens.

I never forgot that kindness.

"I'll miss you." Her voice cracked and my throat pinched.

"I'll miss you too, Amama," I said, and she burst into laughter.

Amara had become a second mama to me, so I called her Amama for a while as a young child and it was what Oslo called her now.

When she pulled back, she was crying. I couldn't remember the last time I'd cried.

"Alright that's enough, you'll soften her too much," Dorian told his wife with a smile and I grinned.

After leaving their hut, I opened the summons again and read it for the tenth time.

To: Mud Flat pack

The royal wolven advisors who serve King Axil are requesting your most dominant female wolven, Zara Swiftwater, to appear at Death Mountain in two weeks' time to enter the Queen Trials.

Winner takes the throne.

Please send your response via courier immediately. A dominant replacement may be sent.

Name of contestant or replacement:

Alpha approval:

I STEPPED inside our house and retrieved a quill and ink from my father's old desk.

Cyrus was silent as he watched me write *Zara Swiftwater* in the contestant's name spot and then *yes* under Alpha approval. I handed it to him.

"Dorian and Morgan will help train me as well," I told him.

He looked impressed at that, and through our pack link I could feel his excitement mixed with apprehension over his little sister entering the trials. As a wolven packmate, there were times when you didn't even need to speak, one could sense the others' thoughts or emotions as if they were your own. And because he was my brother our bond was especially close. As a pack, we could all speak to each other mentally in wolf form but as humans there were just wisps of feelings floating by that you had to intuit.

Cyrus walked over to the storage locker we kept by the couch that had all of my training equipment inside. Flinging it open, he looked at me. "I'll get this to a courier. You get ready, we start right away."

Right away?

"We have two weeks," I pled. Training with my brother was no small feat, he took the task very seriously.

"We should have started six months ago," he growled, and left the room.

I peered over at my little brother, who was watching me from the couch, and tipped my chin high, hoping to look strong and unafraid. When his bottom lip quivered as he tried to hold in his tears, I sighed. He was so much like my mother, always wearing his heart and emotions out in the open. I was more like my father, physically strong, mentally tough and slightly emotionally dead inside. It's just who I was and how I operated. It was a survival technique.

"Listen, kiddo," I told him. "This is the way to bring honor to our family name and to the pack. I will not disappoint us."

Oslo frowned, tucking his knees up to his chest. "I don't care about honor. I just don't want you to get hurt."

I knew in that moment I'd babied him too much and that he was far too soft to survive even midpack. He'd be a submissive like our mother and be relegated to menial tasks within our village, and that saddened me. But maybe that's what he wanted. A life free of hunting and fighting and all the things that got my blood pumping. He was twelve now and this was when your wolf really settled into who they were. A dominant or submissive.

Walking over, I ruffled his hair. "Well regardless, I'll make everyone proud anyway."

It was either that, or a body bag. I wasn't a quitter. I would bend the knee only if it were broken from my leg.

Two weeks had passed and I'd nearly died a dozen times, especially last week on the night of the full moon when my wolf never left her furry form and wouldn't let me transform to human. It felt like Dorian, Morgan and my brother were actively trying to kill me. I was due to leave for Death Mountain in a few moments and my brother wanted one last lesson with me.

"But I've already changed." I motioned to my clean leather trousers and pristine bearin fur coat. Freshly killed last season.

My elder brother glared at me. "You're too clean.

Arrive with blood and dirt on your clothes and it shows how hard you've been working. Make the other women fear you."

He had a fair point. What made my brother the lead trainer for the alpha was this, the mental games he taught people to play in order to win fights.

Get in their head and twist things to distract them or blow them off their game. His advice came back to me.

I sighed and pulled off my fur coat, showing the small strip of fabric over my breasts. As shifters, we went in and out of our wolf form so often it was easier to just tie a strip of cloth over things than to keep ripping expensive tunics.

The members of my village gathered round us, pounding the ground in encouragement.

I grinned: they'd been really supportive of me lately and it meant everything to me to have them standing behind my bid to be winner of the Queen Trials.

I waited for Morgan or Lola to enter the circle and spar with me, but it didn't happen. Instead, the circle opened up and Dorian himself stepped inside, tunic-less and wearing a loin cloth.

Oh Hades.

I'd fought men in our pack before. Small disputes, or for training purposes, but ... never a sparring match with the alpha.

I swallowed hard.

He held my gaze as he entered the circle and instead of protesting or asking what was going on, I cracked my knuckles, preparing for the fight. The pack went wild with howls, even in their human form, and stamped on the ground in excitement.

To my knowledge, the alpha had never sparred with a woman. Probably for fear of killing her.

I could sense my brother's feelings without him having to even speak. We shared a pack link after all.

Dorian was bigger than me, and stronger. So I needed to use my smaller size and speed as an advantage.

The Queen Trials would be a mixture of human fighting, wolf fighting and weapons rounds. I didn't know the details, but I needed to be ready on all fronts.

"Rules?" I asked my alpha as we circled each other. I didn't want to hurt him and have him reprimand me in front of everyone and I also didn't want him to come at me hard if we were just demonstrating technique.

"None," he declared and then launched at me.

A yelp of surprise left my throat but my brother had taught me well. I instinctively dropped to my knees and threw my arm out, connecting my fist with the alpha's groin. He grunted and fell forward, down to my level, and I took him to the ground easily. Yanking his ankle with one hard tug, he fell flat on his stomach. The pack screamed and howled in excitement.

Jumping on Dorian's back, I put one arm around his throat and then tried to use my legs to pin his massive arms down, but it did no good. He stood, with me on his back, and then we were falling backwards. He body slammed me, landing his entire weight on top of me, and the air left my lungs in a rush. I couldn't breathe, my arms going limp as he rolled off me and spun. His fists slammed into my face, stomach, and throat; a barrage assault that was so fast I couldn't get my bearings.

"Use what you have!" my brother snapped.

I felt the dirt beneath my fingers and grabbed a handful, throwing it into the alpha's face. He coughed and sputtered which gave me the chance to catch my breath and roll out from under him.

Time to wolf out. It was the only way I would have a chance. Changing to my wolf form left me vulnerable during the shifting process but he was blinded by dirt for the next several seconds, so it was now or never.

My bones started to snap and transform as the pain ripped through me. Being a shapeshifter and changing forms often didn't make it hurt any less. It was excruciating every time, which naturally had given our kind a high pain tolerance. I was halfway through the shift when Dorian grabbed my leg and pulled.

My upper body hit the ground and then I was being hauled into the air as I completed my shift. I growled and snarled at him but he held me up like a pup as I wiggled and squirmed before him. The pain of shifting made my skin feel raw, but I stayed calm. Dorian landed blow after blow against my stomach, treating me like a punching bag. He wasn't going full steam as this was a sparring match, so my ribs weren't breaking, but I would be bruised pretty good.

In that moment, I remembered everything I'd learned while training with my brother over the years and in the past two weeks.

I suddenly went completely limp, my wolf's head lolling to the side as if I'd passed out.

"Nice try," Dorian snapped and sucker-punched me in the gut again while still holding me up in the air by the leg.

It took every ounce of control I had not to react to the punch. I knew Dorian was a respected fighter who valued honor: he wouldn't ever beat on an unconscious person. It meant he'd already won. It was the one weakness he had, that he was a man of honor and never wanted the easy way out.

With a sigh, he laid me on the ground and addressed the pack. "I guess she—"

I sprang up in my wolf form and went right for his throat, nipping it lightly so that he would know I could have ripped it out had this not been a sparring match. When I landed back on the ground, I looked up to see the red teeth marks I'd grazed across his skin.

I held his gaze as the pack cheered and hollered, knowing I'd won the second I'd nipped his throat. In a real fight, he'd be dead.

Dorian grasped my wolf form by the armpits and hauled me up to stare into his yellow glowing eyes.

"Well done. You're a force to be reckoned with, Zara Swiftwater, you always have been. *Don't* forget that."

It was the Dorian equivalent of *I love you and I am proud of you, kid. Don't die.*

I nodded and he set me down.

With the pack slamming the ground and howling around me, I felt ready to go to the city with my brother.

I made quick work of saying goodbye to Oslo and everyone else. I didn't want to get emotional right before our trip.

"Mind Amara until I've won, and then I'll send for you," I informed my baby bro. She'd already promised to keep an eye on him but twelve was the age of responsibility in our pack. He needed to learn to be on his own. No more babying him.

He gave me a curt nod, his eyes welling with tears and my heart squeezed.

"What if you ... die?" he said as we stood in the doorway of our home.

Cyrus was outside waiting for me, so it was just the two of us.

If he were ten, I'd lie to him and tell him I wasn't going to die. But he needed the truth.

I pulled him into a tight hug. "Then I will miss you the most because you are my favorite," I told him and his arms wrapped around me in a death squeeze. "And you will be fine without me. Be tough and work your way up in the pack until you find a place that feels right."

He nodded against my shoulder and I heard him swallow a sob.

I pulled back from him, not wanting to mother him too much. He was going to have to toughen up if he wanted to survive here without me. But I would be lying if I didn't admit that I wanted to take him with me, to hold him close until he was older and less sensitive.

We were babies when we lost our mother and father. Oslo and I had grown up together. Me and him against the world.

"Get inside and make some lunch for yourself, okay?" I said.

He nodded and wiped at his eyes and that was that. I couldn't linger any longer.

Spinning, I walked over to meet my older brother. He was standing on the wolf sled with half a dozen pack members harnessed and ready to pull it.

If I didn't need to take anything with me, I could have just shifted to my wolf form and walked to Death Mountain, but as a trial candidate with a coach, I needed clothing and weapons and more than my brother and I could carry alone.

"You baby him," Cyrus scolded as I approached.

I rolled my eyes, tired of the same old argument. "Will Mena be okay with the twins while you're gone?" I climbed up beside him on the wolf sled.

His wife Mena had just given birth to twin boys six

months ago; I was sure she wasn't keen on him leaving so soon.

"She'll be fine. She's strong and she's got the pack." He looked around at our small village and I followed his gaze. I loved Mud Flat village. Under the light dusting of snow we had now was an endless sea of cracked mud and there was not a soul for miles and miles. It wasn't for everyone, living out in the middle of nowhere, but I loved the solitude and the company of just our pack. Other packs had to fight for territory but out here, in a place not a lot of people wanted to live, we had hundreds of miles to ourselves. There was nothing more freeing than running at lightning speed across the Mud Flats with no landscape to stop you. We were experts at survival in the elements and I didn't need much to make me happy or comfortable, something I thought would serve me well at the Queen Trials. Rumor had it that in one of the Queen Trials challenges they tested your willpower and tried to wear you down by less than charming living accommodations. The people would not accept a weak queen in any aspect.

Our fellow pack wolves that were tethered to the sled took off then, and I gripped the bars at the sides to hold on. I was weary, covered in dirt and snow and my lip was bleeding but my brother was right. It would be an advantage to show up to the capital looking like this against those posh city wolves.

THE RIDE TOOK all day and part of the evening: we had to stick to the communal trails so that we didn't encroach on any other packs' land. We only arrived at the gates of Death Mountain well after supper time and my stomach was growling. Cyrus had been informed there would be some kind of welcome dinner and then all competitors would be given accommodations for themselves and their coach. I'd never been to Death Mountain. The city held no appeal for me. In the summer I slept outside in a hammock with Oslo so that we could look up at the stars. And even in the winter I went on long daily walks to keep my muscles lean and to stay tolerant against the cold. People in the city didn't do that. They were too good for it, the softest of our kind. Their bodies were plumper and had less muscle definition. Food was brought to them on a platter. Fires were made and stoked for them by servants. Yeah, they could afford all the fancy training coaches but how they thought a strong queen would be chosen from this place was beyond me.

I glanced around as we entered the gates to the city. Death Mountain had been half carved out in an effort to mine for gold by early settlers. So when the wolven took over, they built the palace right on the plateau, halfway up the mountain. There was no army that could reach it without us knowing and throwing them to their deaths before they even got close to us.

We passed a small village of homes that were skinny but tall, some only ten feet wide but four stories high.

Space was in short supply when building on a mountainside.

I stared at the opulent man-made city and felt the thoughts war inside of me. The wolf part of me thought the large lavish stone castle with sparkling gold inlay was a mockery to our kind. We were animals, we slept on dirt, not silk sheets. But the human part of me saw the desire for such necessities. We did spend half the time in these human bodies and they thrived with such luxuries.

The entire front entrance was packed with tents from travelers that had come in from the outlying cities and villages. We had left the wolf sled at the base of the mountain and hiked up together as a pack of eight, all representing the Mud Flats.

Some wolves came out of their tents to assess the newcomers and I made sure to stare each and every one of them down so that they knew their place.

Submissives quickly looked away while fellow dominants held my gaze for longer.

The smell of campfires and cooking meat hit my nose and my stomach growled.

Cyrus looked to the rest of our pack representatives. "Find a place for our tent and set up camp. I have to register Zara inside."

They nodded and one of the more dominant females, Sasha, reached out and squeezed my shoulder. "Make us proud," she told me in serious tone.

I nodded, trying not to let her words have an effect on

me. Representing the Mud Flat pack in the Queen Trials was a huge honor.

Some would say we were the least likely to belong in a palace. We lived off the land, without running water or toilets, like they had in the city and other large towns. We hunted our food, we didn't buy it from market stalls. But I would argue that made me the most likely to win a challenge of this kind. I was hardened by life and I fought every day to keep my place of third in a large pack of ambitious wolves.

As Cyrus and I weaved in and out of the tent city on the large grassy lawn of the palace, people stared and pointed at me. Some even held cards in their hands and marked things on them.

I peered closer at the cards as we passed and my stomach tied into knots.

Betting cards. On who would die first. At first glance it looked like over two dozen names.

Cyrus snapped, causing me to pull my attention to his hands and then he started to speak with his fingers.

Are you nervous to see the king? My brother used hand language to speak to me so that others nearby couldn't understand. One of our packmate's children was born without hearing, which was extremely rare for a wolf, but Tig couldn't even hear the wind rustle. We designed the language in the Mud Flat pack so that we could communicate with him. It also proved useful at festivals and events where we didn't want other packs to hear us with their sensitive ears. In wolf form we could share thoughts, but as humans, this was the best we'd come up with when unable to speak.

No. Why would I be? We were kids when I saw him last. A stupid crush. I moved my fingers quickly and my brother gave me a look that said, 'I don't believe you.' To be honest I wasn't sure I believed myself.

Just don't let anything show on your face. I don't want a weakness exploited by other contestants, he motioned with his fingers.

I nodded once but his words hit me hard.

I wouldn't be affected by seeing Axil Moon ... would I?

THE ROYAL MOON castle was everything I thought a castle would be. Full of servants and electricity and fancy tapestries and more food than I'd ever seen in my life. Cyrus and I had just checked in with the royal wolven advisors who were making sure we followed the rules during the Queen Trials.

"Enjoy tonight. Tomorrow morning the first trial starts," one of the king's advisors said to us.

The advisors were eight in total and descended from a long line of guides to the king. They were easy to spot as they all had shaved heads and wore the red robe that signified their status. Axil was the alpha king, but he did nothing without these men's input.

I nodded curtly and then the advisor looked down at my clothing. "Would you like to be shown to your rooms? You can change before dinner."

Cyrus spoke before I had a chance. "No, we'd like to eat now. It's been a long journey and we aren't concerned with fashion."

The advisor seemed like he'd been slapped and I had to suppress a grin. The psychological warfare had begun. Cyrus was in his element.

"Of course." The man in the red robe gestured to a pair of open doors.

"Oh, I almost forgot. Here is your champion number, Zara." The man handed me a handwritten ticket and I glanced down at it to see the number one written in a big blocky style. There was a pin lanced through it.

The man looked at my chest as if indicating I wear the number. I pinned it on and he nodded in satisfaction.

Judging by the bustling room full of people, I was one of the last women to show up, but had still been given a number one ticket. Interesting. What did it mean? Were we ranked in our rumored abilities or was it just random? Mud Flats didn't get much fanfare and although I was the most dominant female in our pack, I doubted I was the most dominant here.

It would take all the skills my brother had taught me to survive this thing.

As soon as we entered the room, I knew Cyrus had been right to demand I fight our alpha this morning. And to insist we not change our clothes.

The room was full of women in pretty silk dresses that kissed the floor. Their hair was tied up in glossy strands and their combat coaches, whether male or female, were dressed to impress as well.

Every single head turned in our direction when we entered and fear washed over at least half of their faces. Their wild stares ran the length of my blood-encrusted clothing, to the yellowing bruises on my face and stomach, and then to my brother who looked just as hardened from the trip.

Without a word of introduction or nicety we stepped over to a long table and stacked our plates high with meats, potatoes and bread rolls. I tried to take some sweets but my brother swatted my hand.

Fight tomorrow. No sweets, he hand signed.

I wanted to protest, but he was right. My body didn't really like sweets: they felt good going down but always made me sluggish afterward and thirsty the next day if I had too much. We lived off the land in the Mud Flats and other than some wild berries, we didn't have the kind of sweets they had here like cakes and cookies and things they sold at markets in the outlying villages. My body wasn't used to them.

Passing through the crowd which had fallen silent, Cyrus and I looked for an empty table.

As we were walking by, a woman in a green dress with the number three pinned to her top plugged her nose.

"Pee yew, look what the Mud Flats dragged in," she said in a nasal tone. "Clearly she didn't get the memo about—"

I didn't wait for her to finish her sentence; instead I snapped out with a jab to the side of her temple with my free hand and knocked her out cold. Her body crumpled to the floor like a bag of rocks. I looked up at the smartly dressed man who'd been standing next to her as a growl built in his throat. Her combat coach.

"Control your wolf or next time I'll take her arm," I told him.

Fur rippled down the side of his face but he didn't move. I was well within my rights to shut that disrespect down.

Some of the other women gasped in shock at my behavior, but not all of them. One woman, wearing the number two pinned to her gold gown, merely watched me like a hunter watched prey. I needed to set a precedent that I would not take ridicule from anyone, but I realized I had also revealed to the others who their main competition was. Now they would have it out for me.

Oh well.

Cyrus casually took a seat at an empty table as if my outburst was an everyday occurrence and I joined him.

Good girl, he hand signed and I grinned as I began to wolf down my food. I ate like a wild animal, half starved. I had skipped breakfast and lunch and other than snacking on a few strips of smoked meat, this was the only meal I'd had all day.

As I was tearing into a tender piece of elkin meat, a sturdy blonde wearing a blue dress sat next to me. She reeked of floral perfume, which my wolven nose hated, and she wore far too much makeup. The number twenty-four was pinned to her chest.

"Welcome. My name is Eliza Green of Death Mountain pack. I just wanted to take a minute to introduce myself before we all try to kill each other tomorrow." She gave a nervous chuckle.

I said nothing, continuing my meal.

"Wow. You really showed that girl who is boss. I don't even know if we are allowed to start fighting yet, but that was pretty cool," she added.

My gaze flicked up from my food and held her blue eyes as we locked in a stare. I was a good reader of people: this girl was way too nice to survive this thing. And she wasn't being calculating, like trying to make an alliance only to kill me later. That did happen. There was a sweetness in her voice, along with an underlying nervousness. She was innocent.

"I'm probably going to be one of the first to go," she prattled on. "But at least I'll make my family proud, right? Sorry, I talk a lot when I'm nervous."

Cyrus snapped his fingers and I looked at him.

Don't make friends.

I nodded, but I also didn't want this girl to be the first to go.

"Do you want to die tomorrow?" I asked her flatly.

She froze at my words, maybe because it was the first thing I'd said after she introduced herself so nicely.

"Of course not. I want to make my pack proud. This is my home turf," she replied seriously.

I dipped my chin and then leaned in closely. "Then stop being so nice to people. In fact, I want you to spit in the face of the next person that talks to you."

She looked appalled at that and Cyrus reached out and pinched my thigh to stop me from helping her anymore.

"Now *go away*," I snapped and a growl rose in her throat as she stood so fast that her chair fell back and crashed on the ground.

Now everyone was looking at us again.

Good.

I wanted them to remember the face that was going to be the last one they saw before they took their final breath.

I didn't want to kill anyone, but this was our way. The chosen queen must be the strongest among us and that had to be proven in battle.

There was a motion at the front of the room and then everyone quieted and turned their attention that way.

I finished my bite and stood, trying to get a view of what or who they were looking at. The crowd parted and Axil Moon stepped into the room with his older brother

Ansel and two advisors. The moment my gaze fell upon him, it was like I'd been kicked in the stomach. The air knocked out of me, my mouth popped open and it was like I was right back at the training camp all those years ago.

Axil Moon was no longer a boy, he was all man and I wasn't prepared for it.

The sight pulled me suddenly into a memory of our time together at camp.

We'd been inseparable for a month and had gone swimming at the lake with our friends. I splashed the water playfully at fifteen-year-old Axil, causing him to grin, and do the same. I squealed when a ton of water doused my face and hair.

"Too far, Axil!" I growled and took off after him to retaliate. Our friends cheered me on as Axil swam quickly towards the floating tanning dock that bobbed in the center of the lake. We'd all been wrestling and sparring for a month. Axil knew I wouldn't let him live this down without at least getting a good dunk in.

He laughed wildly as I struggled to keep up with him. He was a better swimmer than I was and he knew it. Our friends were now like little blips on the shoreline.

Axil reached the floating dock before me and I kicked harder, wincing when my leg cramped up sharply. I was a decent swimmer, but this lake was really deep and all of a sudden, I had to stop and tread water.

"Axil!" I screamed in panic: my playful anger at him was gone.

He took one look at me floundering and dove into the water, swimming for me harder than a fish.

My leg. Stupid cramp. I tried to keep my head above water, my wolf wanting to come out to protect us.

Suddenly Axil was there, hauling me into his arms. His eyes searched my face frantically. "What happened?" he asked as he pulled us towards the floating dock.

"My leg got a cramp," I told him breathlessly as the panic left my system.

We reached the dock and he hauled me up, and I settled in his lap. He was holding the sides of my face, peering into my eyes with terror.

"I thought ... Zara, I can't ever lose you. I'm in love with you. Now. Forever. Always."

The air was knocked out of my lungs.

"I love you too," I murmured.

Reaching out, he stroked his thumb across my bottom lip and then I leaned forward and captured his mouth with a kiss. He opened his lips to deepen the kiss and our tongues intertwined as I leaned further into him. Since my parents had died, not a lot had made sense in this world. Why bad things happened to good people. Why I'd had such a hard life while others had it easy. But being here now with Axil, wrapped in the safety of his arms, it felt so right. It felt like home.

My brother cleared his throat next to me, pulling me out of the memory and back to the room at Death Mountain. I blushed, giving him an apologetic smile and then looked next to Axil to see Ansel Moon.

His older brother walked with a permanent limp, the only reminder of their fight for alpha king two years ago. Axil had won and now I saw why. He was a head taller than Ansel and bigger too. Axil had a scruffy beard which framed his chiseled jaw and his blue eyes were like arrows seeking flesh as they scanned the room and stopped at me.

I looked away on instinct and found that the woman in the gold dress was watching me with a grin.

Damn. I'd shown my hand, unable to hide that I was affected by seeing the alpha king.

Hopefully she would think I just found him attractive and not that we had a history together.

I could feel Axil's gaze on me and so I took the opportunity to take off my fur coat and showcase my lean chiseled arms and abdominal muscles. I was still just wearing a cloth strip over my breasts and the low-slung tight trousers made of elkin leather. My body was dotted with dried blood, dirt and fading bruises as my wolven healing took care of this morning's wounds. I looked like a warrior, forged in fire and blood, a far cry from the girl he once knew at fifteen.

When I turned to face him, he was passing by our table and looked like he'd seen a ghost. I held his haunted gaze and tipped my chin up high as if to say that I no longer cared that he left me broken-hearted at the training camp all those years ago. I wanted him to think he was barely a memory to me, a wisp in my mind that had all but disappeared.

But I wasn't prepared for the agony that crossed his features. Pure misery was etched into his face and I swallowed hard, trying to process why he would seem that way upon seeing me.

Did he recognize me? I had grown into a woman myself, but I was still the same brown-haired girl he'd asked to dance with at camp.

He walked right up to me and his advisors pushed the crowd of other women back as his brother Ansel began to talk with them, giving us privacy.

I steeled myself for this interaction, for the chance to speak to him after he so cruelly left me without a word.

In every other culture you bowed before kings.

Not ours.

I held his gaze even when it hurt. As my breath hitched, I stared into his blue eyes for as long as possible, as he continued to hold mine in his line of sight. I knew from the moment that I'd met him, when we were fifteen, that he would be a future alpha, but I'd had no idea he was a prince and would one day be the king.

I wanted to show him now that I wasn't the weak little girl from the Mud Flats that he and his brother thought I was back then. And I wanted the first words out of his mouth to be, *I knew it would be you, I knew you would be the strongest among your pack.* I had clawed my way to the top and now I had a chance to be his equal.

"Zara." He breathed my name like a prayer and all rational thought left me. "I don't know whether to be happy you came or horrified."

I paled, not expecting that response. "Horrified? You ... invited me?"

He swallowed hard and then leaned close, his familiar scent washing over me which caused a whine to build in my throat, but I swallowed it down. Lowering his voice to barely a whisper, he pressed his lips against my ear.

"Now I regret it. You shouldn't have come," he said and pulled away from me with a heartbreaking frown before he stalked off, leaving me in a world of hurt and confusion. This was not exactly how I imagined my reunion with Axil, but the bastard had clearly changed. He was no longer the sweet teenage boy I'd tongue kissed for hours under the moonlight while we'd dreamed up a future together.

Horrified to see me? Regretted inviting me? That fool was going to have some regret. I was going to make him regret the day he met me and every day thereafter.

Now I wanted to win this and to become his wife just to deny him every time he asked to bed me.

Wolven mated for life and were monogamous. I'd force the bastard into celibacy as payback for how he treated me.

Never underestimate a woman who'd been scorned.

3

Cyrus and I refused the living accommodations inside the castle and preferred to sleep in the large tent outside with our packmates. After seeing Axil, we'd left and I'd slept in one of the eight hammocks set up inside of the sizeable shelter. I'd much rather have my packmates watching my back while I slept than sleep alone in a room inside the belly of the beast.

To be honest, hearing Axil tell me that I shouldn't have come had shaken me. I felt as unwanted as he'd made me feel all those years ago. I shouldn't allow it to bother me, but it did. After the cruel way he'd broken up with me at camp, to now tell me that I shouldn't have come was awful and I hated him for it. My brain chewed on it all night until I was fuming with rage.

How. Dare. He.

I was quiet all through breakfast as my packmates made a meal of fresh rabbitin and quail eggs they'd hunted that morning.

Cyrus leaned into me, looking across the camp at a familiar woman. She was the one who had been wearing the gold dress the night before.

"Ivanna Rivers. Crestline pack, second in command," he said, and chills ran down my arms. Second? She made second in a pack full of dominant males! Crestline was known for its brutality. A formidable group of wolves who lived in the harshest climate in Fallenmoore. They sometimes got up to six feet of snow in winter and had to go days without food. They were even rumored to eat their own kind in a famine. She would be hardened and probably my biggest competitor.

She too had chosen to sleep in the tent with her pack-mates, a stone's throw from mine. I watched as she and her battle coach walked together to the check-in tent across the lawn. She held my stare the entire time, which stirred my wolf.

"Come on, let's go check in with the red robes," Cyrus said sarcastically, gesturing to the wolf advisors.

I dipped my chin and we both stood as our packmates wished me good luck. I followed my brother over to a check-in table where I was given a blue-colored card by an advisor and told to go to the corresponding colored challenger tent.

"I'll wait for you outside," Cyrus told me. I nodded curtly and stepped into the blue tent.

Ivanna was there, standing in the middle holding a blue card as well. She glared me down as I entered and I moved in a circle around her with predatorial instinct.

She spun to match my movements, never allowing me her back. She was taller than me, and lean, with about the same muscle mass. She was one of the most beautiful women I'd ever seen. Her long dark hair hung down her back in thick glossy curls and her golden skin was riddled with scars up her arms from fighting. It took a lot to scar a wolven. Her chin was perfectly pointed, as was her nose and her pink lips were full and puckered.

There were two tents, red and blue which meant Ivanna and I were not fighting each other. Not today at least. For now, it seemed we were on the same 'team.'

Eliza stepped into the tent then and I noticed how pale she looked. I broke eye contact with Ivanna and glanced at the too-nice wolf.

"We're going to be allowed weapons," the Death Mountain wolf announced with far too much nervousness in her voice.

"Great." I stood and rolled out my neck.

I loved weapons of all kinds. Swords, daggers,

throwing stars, a heavy mace. My blood pumped just thinking about it.

Ivanna stood up straighter, apparently not liking my tall stature next to her.

"I *am* a weapon," Ivanna announced to the tent as more women trickled in. "So I'll pass."

Chills broke out along my arms at her declaration. Did she say that just to get in my head? Or was she really going to pass on the chance to have a weapon?

That was crazy, but also something Cyrus would approve of because it *had* gotten in my head.

Should I pass too? I didn't want to look weak for my first fight, especially not if the king was watching. After our run-in last night, I wanted to show him what he had been missing this whole time.

"King Axil is outside right now, making his way to the combat ring," Eliza said as if reading my mind.

Ivanna and I shared a look and then we were back in a locked stare.

I can do this all day, I thought.

She was clearly looking to see if Eliza's comment had elicited a reaction from me but I stayed completely void of any facial expression.

More competitors filtered into the tent and then one of the wolven advisors to the king strode into the space, wearing his long red robe. Ivanna and I finally broke our stare-down when the advisor stood directly in front of me, forcing me to look up at him. He held a small wooden box with tiny stone replicas of over a dozen weapons.

"Zara, for the Queen Trials you have been ranked in order of dominance. Because you are number one, you may pick first weapon. Once you have chosen, you will go to the weapons tent where they will exchange this with you for the life-sized version."

My heart pounded in my chest at that shocking announcement. So it *was* a dominance ranking. And I'd made number one? How? Ivanna was second in command of her pack. Did Dorian give them an assessment of me or something?

Who cares, I thought to myself.

I knew what Cyrus would counsel me. If Ivanna, who was number two and my biggest competitor, was taking no weapon, then I should pass as well.

"Pass," I said and turned away from the box. A few women in the tent gasped and the advisor stepped closer to me.

"Excuse me?"

I looked him dead in the eyes. "Pass. I don't need a weapon," I told him.

He shook himself as if coming out of a trance and walked over to Ivanna. "Ivanna Rivers, second place. Pick your weapon."

She glanced at me and grinned, and I knew in that moment that I'd been played. Reaching into the box, she pulled out a tiny replica of a nice broadsword and twirled it expertly in her fingers.

"Nice choice," the advisor informed her.

I kept my face completely calm, forced my wolf down and began to twist my dark brown hair between my fingers in mock boredom, as if what she'd just done hadn't bothered me at all. But deep down inside I was furious ... and yet also praising her genius. She'd just gotten the number one pick to go into a fight without a weapon. She could essentially knock me out of the race before it even got started. Without even having to fight me! I wanted to hate her, but she'd earned my respect in that moment.

Eliza sidled up next to me while the other girls chose their weapons and there was a pang of sadness when I was reminded that her number was twenty-four. Probably the last or second to last. City people were weak, it was well-known.

"Any advice?" she whispered to me. "You're such a badass, and I'd love to live through today."

Her eyes swam with tears and I reached out and slapped her hard across the face. She gasped and her wolf surfaced, her pupils threading through with yellow.

People in the tent turned to us but I ignored them. Instead, I grabbed her lightly by the scruff of the neck and pulled her ear to my lips. "Keep your wolf out when fighting in human form. Your human side is too emotional and it will cost you. Fight dirty. Use every angle you have."

She nodded, cinnamon blonde fur rippling down the sides of her face.

"You know who you will be fighting?" I asked her in a low voice.

She dipped her chin. "Number twenty-two."

"No, I mean do you *know* her?"

She seemed to catch on and then nodded again. "Malin Clearwater. Base Mountain pack."

It seemed like the fights were weighted and they'd pit us against someone of a similar strength to us. That was both good and bad news for me. Good because when I killed mine, I'd be taking out a strong member and bad because I'd chosen no weapon.

"What can you use against her?" I questioned, letting go of her neck. "Does she have any weaknesses? Fears? Sick mother, ex-boyfriend, phobias?"

Her eyes widened as if what I'd just mentioned was pure evil but then she nodded. "Her ... her thigh bone broke last year and never fully set right again. She favors one leg. And ... her boyfriend cheated on her this summer."

"Good. What's the name of the girl he cheated with?" I demand. The advisor was almost to her and I knew he'd bring her the crappiest weapon because it would be picked last. A small dagger probably.

"Alessia," she muttered, looking stricken.

"Go in there, ask her how Alessia is doing and then kick out her bad leg, re-breaking her thigh bone," I instructed. I knew I shouldn't be giving her any advice at all and Cyrus would warn against it, but something about her innocence and weakness triggered my dominant desire to protect her.

Her mouth popped open in shock, her wolf retreating as her eyes returned to their normal blue color. She said nothing in response. I could smell the fear on her and I hated that she'd even been chosen to compete. She didn't belong here.

"Do you want to live?" I asked her plainly.

She swallowed hard and nodded and then it was too late to speak any longer. The advisor was here and he held the box towards her with two choices.

A small dagger and a throwing knife.

She looked at me.

"Dagger," I told her and she took the tiny replica of the blade, ready to exchange it in the weapons tent for the larger life-sized version.

The advisor appraised me once again, his hazel-eyed gaze searing right into mine. "Last chance?" He offered me the throwing knife.

I could feel Ivanna's glare burning into me without even looking. If I took this puny weapon, she won.

I shook my head and he snapped the box shut.

"Everyone follow me," he stated and walked out of the tent.

As a group we stepped out into the sunlight in a single file line and followed the advisor. The entire front lawn of the palace was jam-packed with wolves from all over the realm, but they parted as we passed.

"Go, Mud Flat pack!" someone screamed and I couldn't help a grin. I recognized the voice as one of my packmates.

"Wash Basin pack!" another chanted.

"Eagle Cliff pack!" More chants and then howls and pretty soon the crowd was deafening, cheering on their favorite contestant or packmate.

When we reached a large open area that had been roped off into a circle, my eyes searched for Axil. The king. A little jolt of electricity ran through me as I found him already watching me. He was wearing a red silk tunic, unbuttoned at the chest. The sun shone on his tan skin as he sat upon a raised throne that looked out over the fighting area.

At the sight of him and the fighting ring, again I was pulled into a memory of our summer together.

"Axil Moon, you are up to spar. Pick your opponent," Coach Varryl had said.

It was the second day of camp, and although Axil and I had spent the previous night dancing and kissing, I didn't know if that was just a one-night thing. All of the students stood in a ring around the thick foam mats where the wrestling match was about to begin and Axil walked slowly past each person. Some of the males growled at him as if begging him to pick them. I hoped he wasn't one of those guys who wouldn't spar with a girl because he was afraid of hurting her. I wanted him to know I wasn't delicate. When he passed me, I stepped out of line and right up to him, tipping my chin up as if to say, choose me.

The lopsided grin he gave me was so enticing my legs went weak.

"I choose Zara Swiftwater."

I tied my long hair up and handed my shoes to a friend before going to stand before Axil on the mats. My heart raced as we walked around each other, sizing the other up. I could feel the dominance coming off of him in waves. His gaze was difficult to hold for too long, though not impossible, and I felt that for him to really want to be with me, he had to know I was strong.

The coach blew his whistle and I charged forward, sweeping my leg out and pulling Axil off his feet. He went down with a grin and I leapt on top of him, straddling his waist as our friends and fellow campgoers went wild with cheers. The moment I positioned myself on top of him he bucked upward with his pelvis and grabbed my arms, throwing me to the side and then reorienting himself so that he was now on top of me. It happened so fast I could barely track it. He was sitting on my ribcage, pinning my arms down, and the screaming of excitement around us was deafening.

"It's okay to tap out," he teased.

"Never," I growled and a fire lit in his eyes.

But he had underestimated my flexibility. Because he was sitting on my ribcage and not my pelvis, I was able to *throw my legs upward and cross my ankles in front of his neck, pulling him backwards off of me. He went down hard and I rolled away, taking him into a chokehold. I thought for sure he was going to tap out but he reached up and pried my arms away from his neck.*

I growled in frustration and then he flipped over, reaching down to pick me up, tossing me over his shoulders like a scarf. The crowd went wild as Axil walked over to the coach.

"Call it off," he begged. "She's my future wife and I can't hurt her."

All of the girls at camp gave a collective 'aww' and I couldn't help but grin. Axil was a charmer and I was fully under his spell.

The coach blew his whistle and gave us both a little chuckle.

"Young love," he muttered.

Now I forced myself to push away the memory and look away from Axil, not liking the effect he had on me and not wanting Ivanna to get wind of our past romance.

The grassy fighting area was quite large, big enough for us to shift into our wolf form and run circles around our opponent without feeling squished.

The red-tent fighters lined up around the edge of the rope opposite us, then the king stood and cleared his throat.

"We've long held the belief that a queen does not deserve to serve next to her king unless she is the strongest among us!" he shouted and the surrounding wolves chanted and howled their agreement.

"Just as I fought my way into this spot, my future queen must do the same!" He gestured to his brother, whom he'd nearly killed to become king, and again was met with excitement from the crowd. I watched his brother's face, the clenched jaw and fisted hands, and knew he was not over the defeat. Why Axil let him live I would never know. It was rare that two brothers fought and one forfeited. It made me think Axil had a soft spot where his older brother was concerned.

And soft spots were weaknesses.

"This first fight will help us whittle down the numbers of our strongest warrior women. Although we *do* allow all fights to end in forfeit, it is frowned upon—" The crowd booed loudly and Axil chuckled.

Yeah, they allowed forfeit, but then your pack tore you to pieces for shaming them in such a way. I would rather perish than yield in the Queen Trials. The dishonor I would carry would kill me if I survived.

"You should be ready to die for your people, as I am," Axil added when the crowd quieted.

"Thank you, my lord." One of the advisors spoke loudly as he stood next to the king on the raised platform.

"Here are the rules!" the advisor bellowed. "Stay within the roped-off area. You must enter the fight in your human form but may shift. Use only the weapon assigned to you. The fight starts when the bell rings. That is all!"

The wolves around us wasted no time in chanting, "Fight, fight, fight!"

The lead advisor walked over to Eliza and then to the woman I assumed was Malin and beckoned them both into the ring.

They were starting with the weakest fights first.

I reached out and yanked Eliza's wrist, forcing her to look at me. "Make it fast, element of surprise."

She gulped and nodded. I hoped she took what I'd said to heart. I knew it was cruel; I didn't relish exploiting someone's weakness but if she wanted to survive, she would have to fight dirty.

Eliza wore a fancy city warrior's get-up, full leather armor with padded arms and shoulder spaulders. It was something that would tangle up if she shifted into her wolf form. Eliza gripped her dagger tightly in her hand and I could already see from the way that she hefted the weapon that she was probably an expert swordswoman. All of the Death Mountain high society women were. But they wouldn't last a day out in the outskirts, or in a real fight with few to no rules.

Eliza circled the other girl, who I saw now was holding the same dagger. Good, they were well matched.

"How is Alessia?" Eliza asked Malin and the woman's eyes bugged wide at the mention of her ex-boyfriend's lover. She was beautiful, honey-blonde hair, green eyes, and right now, wearing a feral snarl.

The bell dinged and Eliza lunged forward with more

speed than I thought she'd have. With her left boot she reeled back and came crashing down on Malin's right thigh bone. At the same time Eliza slashed at Malin's face with her dagger.

The sound of crunching bone rang throughout the space and the crowd went insane. A small bit of pride welled in my chest for Eliza. She was a good student; she'd done everything I had said.

Malin fell to the ground wailing in pain and dropped the hold on her weapon. Eliza kicked it away quickly and I knew what would happen next. It's what I would do.

Yes, our magic allowed us to regenerate wounds but we couldn't make more blood if we lost it too quickly.

Eliza took Malin's moment of weakness and slashed at her opponent's throat until crimson lifeblood leaked down her tunic.

Malin reached up to staunch the wound but it was too late.

She keeled over and then the surrounding wolves began to chant Eliza's name.

It was one of the fastest kills I'd ever seen.

I couldn't help but grin. I barely knew this girl and yet I was proud of her; she had won her first fight on her home turf. It must feel good. She spun to me, wearing a matching smile and I tipped my head to her.

Then she turned to the king and gave him a smile with a wink and my pride for her died in my chest and slid into my stomach like a rock. Jealously flared to life inside of me but I pushed it away. I shouldn't care, I hated Axil.

That emotion was a weakness that could be exploited and I needed to remember every woman here was competing for the king's heart, and to be his beloved.

The next fight played out, and then the next and the next. It was going in order of strength and getting more brutal as time went by. I knew my brother and packmates were close by but it wasn't until I was next to be called up that Cyrus appeared.

"Where is your weapon?" he asked, looking down at my empty hands.

"Long story." I glared at Ivanna who had just entered the fighting ring.

He stood next to me as the bell rang and we watched her together. She was my strongest competition and now I saw why. Her fighting style was vicious and perfect. Every punch connected with a main organ or broke a bone. Every swipe of her sword tore at a ligament. She even partial-shifted one paw to swipe at her rival's face which was really hard to do. Partial-shifting was like holding your breath for a really long time. It took skill.

By the time she killed number four in rank, she had gained my respect as a fighter and I knew that if she bested me, she would make a strong queen.

I was trying not to steal glances at King Axil but it was hard since every time I did, he was staring back at me. Was

I just catching him staring every time or was he spending the entire time looking at me?

Surely not.

Right?

"Okay, we have the final match for today!" the advisor announced. "Our number one competitor, Zara Swift-water of the Mud Flat pack, who has chosen not to take a weapon—"

The king growled then, loudly, and some people turned to look at him.

"Can she do that?" Axil asked, disrupting the advisor and scowling at me.

The advisor looked affronted at the interruption. "Of course she can, my lord."

Charcoal black fur rippled down Axil's neck and I frowned.

What the Hades did he care? I knew he and his brother would rather I died quickly so they didn't need to worry about my polluting their bloodline with mud. As Ansel had so aptly said five years ago when he was king.

"And our number three competitor, Arin Moonlight of Wash Basin pack, fighting with the long sword!"

Cheers and clapping rang out through the space and I grinned as I stepped into the ring.

Arin was the same woman who had told me I stank last night and I'd knocked her out.

"Did you have a nice floor nap last night?" I asked her.

She snarled, baring all her teeth and holding her sword aloft.

I could feel Axil's gaze on me but forced myself to push him from my mind.

The bell rang and instead of exploding forward like I usually would, to catch her off guard, I ran backwards all the way to the edge of the rope.

She frowned, as if confused by my behavior.

I had no weapon, she had a three-foot sword. I wasn't stupid. Rushing her would get me stabbed and although I would eventually heal, it would take time. I had no idea if the next fight was in an hour, or tomorrow morning, so keeping my guts in my stomach was top priority.

I kept my hands behind my back and had decided that since Ivanna had showed off with her partial shift, I would as well.

In the time that I had run backwards and confused her, causing her to advance towards me, I'd already shifted both of my hands into giant, razor-sharp paws. It took incredible skill to hold onto a shift like this and I would be partially distracted in order to keep the rest of my body from taking my wolf form as well. To do a full shift would put me in a vulnerable space and she would probably cut my head off before I was on all fours.

"Come on, you coward!" Arin came down and across with her sword, going right for my neck. When the blade was a few inches from my body, I swiped out with a paw and crashed into the side of the sword. The force of the blow was far greater than my human form could muster and too much for her grip. The weapon clattered to the ground and she let loose with a battle cry as she lunged for me. Both of her hands wrapped around my throat as she tried to yank me to the ground in a fit of anger.

She was too emotional, all anger and no calculated skill. Reaching out with my paw, I swiped at the side of her face, taking a strip of flesh with it. Her fingers released from my neck as her wail of pain tore through the space and she stumbled backwards. Shifting my paws back to hands, I reached down and picked up her fallen sword.

By the time she realized what I'd done, I'd already slammed the sharp end into her heart.

The crowd roared their approval and as I looked at her dead body, I thought I would feel pride ... but I didn't. Instead, I felt slightly ashamed. I knew it was our custom and fighting for pack dominance had always been the way, but to shame women for forfeiting to keep their life was a mistake. Arin didn't have to be lying dead at the end of my blade, she could have taken a knee if she had known there was no shame in that, and that her pack would let her live. I looked into the blank stare of Arin's dead eyes and I realized I was fighting for a man I didn't even want anymore, and a crown I wasn't sure I was worthy to wear.

It felt wrong.

My brother leapt into the ring and lifted me into the air in praise, snapping me from my stupor and I looked over at the king.

Gone was his earlier anger, instead Axil was staring at me with compassion. Like he'd seen something on my face that told him I wasn't feeling so great about things right now.

"Put me down," I growled to my big brother. Cyrus stiffened beneath me and dropped me as the crowd went wild.

I turned from him suddenly and ran out of the ring, pushing past the crowds of people until they thinned and then I was walking among the hundreds of tents.

Why was I here? Why the Hades did I sign up for this? Was it to see Axil again and prove to him I was everything he needed and that he never should have left me all those years ago? Or was it really to bring pride to my pack? Was I killing other women just to get my revenge on Axil Moon?

Feeling confused, I just kept walking, wanting to blow off some of the adrenaline from the fight. My walk turned into a jog and before I knew it, I was full-on sprinting. I loved to run. Human, or wolf form, it didn't matter. The wind was in my hair, my muscles crying for release and my breath heaving. I needed this. I blasted past the melee of the crowds and when I hit the castle, I turned right and went around it to see what was behind. I was rewarded with a thick forest that stretched out for a couple hundred feet before going off a sharp cliff down the mountain.

My legs burned in the good way only a heavy workout could bring as I hit the treeline and kept going. Dodging trees and heavy brush, I ran right up to the edge of the mountain and stopped.

My chest heaved as I peered over the cliff below and then I heard a twig snap behind me.

I spun, throwing my arms up as I readied myself for a sneak attack from Ivanna. Take out the competition before you even had to fight them. It's what I would do.

But when I saw Axil stalking towards me, my arms dropped and my mouth popped open a little in surprise.

"I wasn't fleeing. I just needed some time alone," I told him in case he thought I might be running from my obligation. Because that's what this was, an obligation. If Dorian hadn't sent me, we'd have had to choose a replacement. Each pack sent one female no matter how weak they were. Like Eliza. The sweet girl who was so unprepared that she was asking fellow contestants for advice on how to keep her life. It made me sick.

He didn't stop walking, and I swallowed hard when he got within two feet of me before slowing.

I held my breath as he stepped right up to me, toe to toe and stared me down. His nostrils flared and I had to suppress a moan. He smelled like dominance and bad choices, like fifteen-year-old Axil. The memory of kissing him was burned on my tongue and I suddenly wondered if he tasted the same.

"You didn't take a weapon? I remember you being smarter than that, Zara," he growled and that anger was back in his gaze.

I placed one hand on my hip. "I'm surprised you remember me at all with how easily you left me," I snapped back, though I wasn't sure it was true. One of the things he'd said to me was that he would never forget a single freckle on my skin. He'd traced them nightly under the stars all summer.

"I ..." His face fell. "Zara, leaving you—"

"I don't want to talk about that. The past is the past." I pursed my lips.

He looked down at his hands for a second and then back up at me. "Look ... Zara, I've been thinking, you could break your leg. Say it happened hiking and I would excuse you from tomorrow's trial. Dorian could send a replacement."

My glare narrowed as rage built up inside of me. "Are you *that* afraid of me winning and being stuck with me the rest of your life?" My head tipped back as genuine laughter erupted from my throat.

When I looked back at him, his anger was completely gone and his eyes were on my lips.

"Damn, I forgot how sexy your laugh was."

His words knocked the air from my lungs and I froze as he leaned forward and against my neck, inhaling deeply.

"But I remembered how good you smelled." His voice was ten octaves deeper.

My mind was scrambling to figure out what was going on when his fingers came up to brush across my lips. The whimper I'd been holding in released then and he pulled back to look at me.

"And for as long as I live, I will *never* forget how you kiss, Zara Swiftwater," he stated and my legs nearly collapsed beneath me. "And I *dream* of being stuck with you forever, I don't fear it."

There were no words for this moment. I didn't have anything to say so I just stared at him. Why was he muttering all of these incredibly romantic things to me? He left me at the summer camp after his brother reminded him of his duties to the throne. I was Mud Flats trash, not good enough for him.

The memory of how that all went down rose up inside of me and I took one step closer to him so that my body was pressed flush against his. My breasts slammed into his chest and his eyes widened slightly.

"Axil Moon, I pray that you remember how I kiss, for the rest of your life." I leaned in and dragged my lips lightly across his, delighted to hear the moan of pleasure escape him. Then I pulled back and met his gaze. "Because you will *never* taste this mouth again. I will win the trials, become your wife, and leave you to an empty bed until my dying day."

With a snarl of anger, I pulled away and sidestepped him, walking quickly back through the woods the way I came.

I thought I heard the sound of snapping bones and

when I reached the open grassy knoll behind the castle, a tortured howl rose up across the forest behind me.

Whatever he was feeling now was an ounce of what my fifteen-year-old self had felt when he rejected me.

Now, more than ever, I was motivated to win this competition. If nothing more than to see the look on Axil's face when I slammed the bedroom door shut on him on our wedding night. I didn't care who I would have to kill to get my revenge. This was our way, and I'd been stupid to question such traditions.

4

The next morning I hurriedly washed up at the outdoor communal bathhouse and then put on fresh clothes. Cyrus said that he'd gotten drunk with one of the king's advisors last night and that they had let slip that the next trial was one I was well suited for, living in the Mud Flats, but I might have to go hungry for a few days. Going without meals didn't worry me, unless of course I was weakened and then called into a fight, which was probably going to happen. They were testing our strength. So instead of the light breakfast I normally ate, I scarfed meat and fresh fruits until I was sickeningly full.

When I arrived at the blue champion tent, it hit me that there were only twelve of us left.

How quickly we'd been culled in half shocked me but I got over it quickly when Ivanna gave me a grin.

She was no doubt still basking in her ability to have made me take no weapon into my fight yesterday.

I walked right up to her and looked her in the eyes. "I still won," I reminded her.

Her gaze narrowed but she said nothing.

"Hello champions!" a familiar voice called behind me and I turned to see the same male advisor from yesterday. He was holding a large canvas sack and held it out to us. Eliza slipped into the large tent last, looking sleepy and possibly like she'd been up all night crying. I wondered whether yesterday was her first kill and how she was taking it.

"Place any weapons or personal items, other than clothing that you have on, in here." He shook the bag.

We all looked at each other in confusion.

"You will be searched," he added and that got us moving.

I reached down into my boot and pulled out my small knife. Ivanna did the same and some of the others too.

Eliza took a fancy jeweled hair clip from her blonde tresses and held it up. "Will I get it back?" she asked and I rolled my eyes.

This girl was begging to die.

"Of course," he said as she dropped it warily in the

bag. He cinched it shut and then tossed it onto the ground in the corner of the tent. "For the next trial you will be blindfolded and dropped off at an unknown location."

A few gasps caused him to nod. "You must make your way back here to basecamp, living off the land to keep you alive. A queen of the wolven needs to be able to live off the land."

My attention immediately went to Eliza and I watched as the blood drained from her face and she swayed a little on her feet. This wasn't a normal Queen Trials challenge. At least not in any of the ones I'd heard about.

This was it. This was how she died. Wet, cold, and with no food in her belly as a giant cougarin split open her gut while she slept. I sighed when she looked at me in terror.

Don't make friends.

My brother's words bounced around my skull and I tore my attention away from her.

Two wolven guards entered the tent then and patted us down for hidden luxuries that might make our wilderness survival any easier. They took my leather strap belt which only caused me to roll my eyes. I could go into the challenge naked and still fare better than Eliza and most of the others.

Ivanna was from Crestline pack and I knew she would have knowledge of how to survive the elements. Olesa too. I'd met her yesterday and come to find out she was from

Upper Rim pack. It was better weather than Crestline, but they weren't as modernized as the other packs.

Everyone else was screwed. The other nine girls were from cities or villages that were extremely spoiled, with market stalls to buy their food from. I could guarantee none of them had so much as picked a piece of fruit from a tree their entire life. Or skinned a bearin.

When we were completely stripped of anything of use, we were called out of the tent. The crowd cheered wildly at the sight of us and we made our way to a set of three wolf sleds. My gaze flicked around the crowd until they landed on my brother.

Find water first, he hand signed.

I nodded.

Make alliances. Assassinations possible, he added and my stomach dropped.

Of course. Ivanna could cut my throat in my sleep and say I died of a bearin attack.

I nodded again to indicate I understood him.

Relief spread through my chest as I realized I would be able to help Eliza without feeling like I was betraying my brother's command not to make friends. I snaked my arm out and grasped her hand, pulling her next to me.

She looked terrified and when I drew her to me, she peered at me expectantly.

I hung back with her a few paces as all the others walked ahead of us and I was sure the roaring crowd was too loud for anyone to hear.

"Do you want to have an alliance? I can help you survive the elements if you take watch while I sleep. We can rest in shifts," I said quickly.

Relief washed over her face and she squeezed my hand. "Yes. I didn't want to die on my birthday."

I stilled. "Today is your birthday?"

She nodded shyly.

A sickly feeling washed over me then. She shouldn't be here. Why was she even put forward for this fight? She was too sweet. Dominant yes, but too loving and innocent and all the crap you needed to *not* be in order to survive these trials.

"Well, this is the shittiest birthday party I've ever been to," I commented and she barked out in laughter, which made her look like a young teenage girl.

"Thanks. I needed that."

I inclined my head and we carried on, following the others onto the backs of the sleds. A troupe of guards stepped over to us and the king was among them. They all held thick strips of cloth to bind our eyes. The guards approached each woman and I steeled myself when the king approached me.

Reaching up, he covered my eyes with the blindfold and his arms rested on the sides of my neck.

'You will be going north.' Axil's deep voice infiltrated my mind and I gasped slightly. Of course. He was king now and as such had all of the powers of the king wolven. Mental communication in human form while touching skin was one of them.

'*You will be deep in the dead lands with no trees or bushes for shelter. No small game or berries for food. The only water you will find is inside of the round bulbous plant that looks dead but is not.*'

Whoa. What?

'*Why are you telling me this?*' I sent the mental message to him and hoped it was received.

I felt his fingers trail against my neck then, very briefly as he slowly pulled away from me. '*Because the thought of you not coming back makes me forget how to breathe.*'

He was gone then, his footsteps retreating with the other soldiers.

I was angry in that moment. Axil Moon was breaking the rules to help me and it wasn't fair to the others. Not only that, but he was acting like he wanted me to win this thing and that really infuriated me. He had his chance with me when we were fifteen. He had said no and dug his grave, so now I was going to make him lie in it.

The sled lurched forward and I reached out and grasped onto the handle as Eliza yelped beside me. Cold hard wind slapped at my face and arms for hours and I couldn't get what Axil just did out of my head. He gave me inside information because he thought I was too weak to win this on a level playing field? That wasn't fair! And it pissed me off. Don't speak to me for five years and then summon me to fight as your wife, then tell me you regretted inviting me and *then* give me information to help me win? This man was a mess! What was he thinking?

We rode all morning, all afternoon and into the early evening. The frigid chill in the air turned to a warmth that was only possible in the dead lands. The dead lands spanned a large part of our territory and backed up to the Nightfall border and the coast of the sea. It was a weird corner of our realm that got a blast of warm sea air and harsh sunlight so nothing grew out here.

The dead lands ran for hundreds of miles, so even knowing where we were told me nothing. But knowing we'd gone north inside the dead lands told me I had to go south to get back to Death Mountain. I stewed over the unfairness of the king telling me all of this information until the sleds finally stopped.

"Get off!" a guard snapped and I backed up off of the sled. "Don't move!" he ordered and then I heard a loud thump, like a body falling onto the floor.

"What was that?" someone asked and then another thump.

Thump. Thump. Thump. One after the other I heard the sound of my fellow competitors being disarmed and all I could do was brace myself.

A cold rag came over my mouth and I didn't even fight it. I breathed in a huge lungful of a pleasant smelling aroma as wooziness washed over me and then everything went black.

Thump.

"DON'T TOUCH HER!" Eliza snarled and I sat bolt upright, just in time to see Ivanna stalking towards me with a sharpened rock in her hand. Dizziness washed over me as the effects of whatever drug they had used fled from my system. Eliza was crouched in front of me, and the sound of snapping bones filled the open air. She was shifting to protect me and honor our alliance. Had she not, I might already be dead.

Now that Ivanna saw I was awake she faltered and I stood, a little unsteady, but fisted my hands ready to fight.

There were half a dozen girls still passed out on the ground and three more were off in the distance, scattered and running in different directions. It was bright out, morning by the position of the sun. We'd slept all night.

It was a miracle nothing had eaten us; the dead lands were known for being full of bearin.

Muffled moans and groans began to ring out as the other women woke up. Ivanna and I were locked in a stare and I grinned maniacally. "We can do this now if you want," I told her, cocking my head to the side.

I would enjoy killing Ivanna: she had no honor if she was going to bludgeon me with a rock while unconscious. She'd lost any respect she had gained from me.

Eliza had fully shifted into her wolf form now and I was surprised at how big she was. She stood a good head taller than my wolf and looked thicker too. Her lips peeled back into a snarl as she growled at Ivanna.

"But you might have trouble fighting us both." I smiled.

Ivanna swallowed hard, dropping the rock and putting her hands up in a playful gesture. Now that all of the other girls were awake and looking around at the vast open land, I didn't feel right about having the knowledge Axil had given me and keeping it to myself.

"My brother got drunk last night with someone who gave him inside information," I told them all. "They took us north, into the dead lands. No food will be found and the only water comes from a bulbous plant that looks dead." Was that everything? I couldn't remember.

"Why are you telling us?" one girl asked, standing unsteadily.

I shrugged. "I want to win on an even playing field."

"She could be lying," Ivanna mused, her dark hair slicked into a nice bun, as she glared at me. "Her brother is a master at mental manipulation. This could be a trick to get us to head south and not waste time looking for food."

I rolled my eyes. "Suit yourselves." Reaching down, I grabbed the clothes Eliza had dropped before shifting and picked them up. She might need them later. Then I tapped on her shoulder and started a brisk walking pace to the south. I would bet my lucky hunting knife none of the city girls knew which way south was. They could probably smell their home in wolf form if we'd only traveled for an hour or two out, but at my estimation we'd trekked twelve hours on a briskly paced wolf sled which meant we were probably two days from making it home on foot. *If* we didn't get lost. The lack of food would slow our pace and if we didn't find water it would affect our stamina as well. The other three girls who'd gone off in all directions would be stuck out here for a week and eventually succumb to the elements.

Eliza stayed in her wolf form, which I actually thought was smart. "You're a really big wolf. You should do all the rest of your fights in wolf form if you can manage to shift fast enough." Now I saw why her name had been thrown into the ring for top contender. She was as big as the male wolves which was a huge advantage when fighting a smaller female.

She looked up at me and gave me a wolfish grin, appearing to like my compliment.

"And thanks for having my back just now. I owe you one," I added as she happily trotted beside me.

I peered behind me to see that the girls had gathered into a little group and seemed to be arguing about something. Probably whether or not to believe my advice. That wasn't my problem. I told them what I knew and pretty soon they would realize it.

"We need to find water. Let me know if you see any plants, even if they look dried up and dead," I told Eliza.

She immediately put her snout to the ground and took

off ten paces ahead of me to the south, sniffing the dirt like a tracker wolf.

We would need to pace our return to Death Mountain and because of the dense fog in the distance, I couldn't see anything beyond a few miles. We could go without food but needed water.

After walking for an hour, I turned around and saw four blobs in the distance behind me, following my trail. It seemed at least four of the girls had believed what I'd told them. The others would be dead if they didn't figure it out soon. I couldn't tell if one of the blobs was Ivanna.

Eliza's wolf yipped in high-pitched excitement and I spun back to face her. There on the ground between the cracks of earth and dead dry brush were strands of a long dead plant that had little balls attached to the vine. It reminded me of sea kelp.

Exhilaration thrummed through me as I crouched closer. The plant was covered in a white powder which made it appear to have no signs of life but when I picked it up, I grinned. It was heavy and the white powder was coming off on my fingers, revealing a dark green healthy bulbous fruit-like plant beneath.

Squeezing one of the bulbs between my fingers, I laughed when fresh clear water squirted out.

Eliza turned in a circle as if chasing her tail and I scooped up a giant six-foot string of the plant and ripped it from the ground, putting it around the back of my neck to travel with like a scarf.

Eliza whimpered and looked up at me.

I shook my head. "We don't need it just yet. Let's ration in case we don't find any more."

I was thirsty too but not desperately so.

City wolves. I shook my head.

After a few more hours of walking, we'd discovered ten more vines. I was now easily popping the bulbs into my mouth after brushing off the tasteless powder and sucking down the cool liquid. The roots must have run really deep into an underground water reservoir because they were full of fresh water. I gave Eliza's wolf plenty as well and we had more than enough for the walk out of here stored around my neck in heavy hanging vines.

I couldn't help but think where we would be if Axil had not told me about them ... his blue eyes, the things he'd said to me over the past two days. They swirled around my head, leaving me in a wave of confusion.

We walked south at a decent pace until the sun started to lower in the sky and my legs felt like mush and my body craved rest. A wolven shifter could go without food for about seven days but it cost us a lot of energy. Especially if we were shifting forms like Eliza had. I knew by the way she was walking, her back legs giving out, that she needed rest.

"We'll camp here tonight." I pointed to a cropping of three dead bushes that would give us zero protection against predators or the elements. It was just an easy spot to point to. She walked over to the dried bushes and collapsed in front of them panting and then looked at me as if awaiting the next instruction.

"You can sleep first. I'll wake you in a few hours for my turn," I told her.

At that declaration her head dropped onto the dry mud and she closed her eyes. She was out.

I peered at the ground around our little camp before the sun was totally blotted from the sky and found a few smooth rocks and a large stick. Useless as weapons if we were attacked.

I didn't want to shift into my wolf form and consume the energy, especially without food, which was why Eliza was staying a wolf. She'd already done it once and to go back and forth would kill her of starvation quicker. We both knew that without even saying it.

I was confident Axil hadn't lied to me and I was sure we were going south. What I questioned was whether we would get lost or slow down so much that it took us longer to reach Death Mountain than I had anticipated.

My mind warred with my instinct as I tried to do the math on when I last ate. We had spent twelve hours traveling here on the wolf sled, and then twelve hours knocked out. Then another twelve hours walking today. Yesterday morning with Cyrus was my last meal. So almost two days.

If I shifted into my wolf form to keep us safe from predators overnight, the walk tomorrow would be slower because I might have to shift back to human form to carry the long and heavy water bulbs. Draping them over my wolf's back might only cause them to fall off as I walked on all fours and had no boxy shoulders to keep them on.

A howl rose up in the distance and my instinct won. Pushing the wasted energy and the future lack of food from my mind, I stripped down quickly and fell onto all fours as my body welcomed the change. Some wolves didn't like being in their animal form more than a few hours, others could go days without changing shape.

I was the latter, most dominants were. I loved being in my powerful wolven form. And if I shifted now, I'd probably have to remain this way or I might not have the energy to shift back to human.

It didn't matter what my mind thought, though, as I'd already started the change. Muscles strained, bones broke and I breathed through the pain.

Eliza lifted her head to look at me sleepily, probably awoken by the noise but then dropped back down when she realized I was just doing this as a precaution and we weren't under imminent threat.

Once my shift was complete, I felt so much better. If a threat were to pose itself somewhere in the night, I would be ready to fend it off.

I was tired but I didn't want to fall asleep, so I stayed standing. Every half hour or so I took a small loop around sleeping Eliza to keep my blood pumping and force myself to stay awake and alert. I was bored and so I allowed my mind to wander to the time I'd first met Axil.

I never wore dresses but my friend Maxine had

convinced me to wear one to the skills camp registration day. It was mostly a meet and greet with the other dominants. The dress I'd worn was white with small pink flowers embroidered on it. Way too girly for my usual style and yet I'd felt beautiful in it. A lot of teenagers went to the summer skills camp in Eagle Cliff territory to hook up and I had hoped to find a boy with whom I could share my first kiss, but I'd had no idea I would meet the love of my life.

I was fifteen, dominant and incredibly naive.

After registration, I'd made my way to the food tent. There was a full band set up and as the sun set on the first night, I was dancing my heart out with Maxine. My arms were up in the air as I threw my hips side to side and laughed with a carefree joy I hadn't had since my parents died.

That's when Axil made his move.

The first thing that attracted me to him was his confidence. Most dominant men had an annoying level of confidence but Axil's was tempered with something else. Something I couldn't put my finger on at the time.

Respect. He respected me even before he'd touched my hips and stepped in front of me, looking down at me with those piercing blue eyes.

"Dance with me." It was more of a command than a question but I knew I could say no if I'd wanted. He was the most handsome boy I'd ever seen, so I nodded and threw my arms around his neck.

That's when he leaned forward and smelled me. His

nose went to my hair and he moaned. I'd never met such a forward boy in my life! These things were not done at a first meeting in my pack, but with him ... it felt right.

"What do I smell like?" I asked him with all the innocence of my fifteen-year-old self.

He pulled back and said something I'd never forgotten. Something that still plagued me today.

"My future wife." He grinned.

In that moment, I'd fallen instantly in love with him. A puppy love with no depth but it was love just the same. First love. The reckless, careless kind that you jump into without much thought or fear of consequence.

I was the first to kiss him. Right there on the dance floor after he told me I smelled like his future wife. I captured his mouth in mine and our tongues danced. We alternated between kissing and dancing for hours until the camp organizers finally told us to head back to our tents.

The camp was a two-month long event and Axil made me promise to meet him the next day.

I did. And we'd fallen deeper. After our classes he took me to the river and we went fishing and talked until the sun went down. I told him all about my childhood and he shared some things but never about being a prince.

On the fifth week of the camp, he braided some string together and slipped it over my ring finger. He promised to one day make me his wife. He said that he had to go back to Death Mountain and deal with family business but when he was a man, he would send for me. Dorian didn't allow us to get married until we were seventeen at the youngest anyway, so I knew I would have to bide my time to get my alpha's permission.

I nodded enthusiastically. I would have agreed to anything, I was head over heels in love with him. We both planned to meet at the next skills camp the following year and then we spent the rest of the night dancing.

We snuck away from our pack tents that night and met on a blanket under the stars. We didn't have sex, we just wanted to fall asleep next to each other. We did this for the last two weeks of camp, sneaking out of our tents and falling asleep together under the stars. And that's how his older brother Ansel, the king at the time, found us the next morning.

Nausea and anger roiled through me as the painful scene flashed through my mind. The way his brother talked about me like I was trash. The way Axil said nothing to defend me. How he'd cowered to his brother and walked away without even looking at me. It made me sick and then I never saw him again.

I went to the next skills camp at sixteen, fully planning on dancing with another guy to make Axil jealous, but he never showed.

That bastard broke my innocent little heart into a thousand pieces and I'd never loved since. I'd had two boyfriends, but saw each of them as someone to warm the bed, not a person I could envision a life with. My heart felt raw for five years and never healed enough to let anyone in again.

Now here I was, fighting to be Axil's wife. The irony was not lost on me.

Eliza rustled next to me then and I pulled myself from my thoughts. She stood, shaking herself and then indicated with her head that I should lie down.

If we were packmates we'd be able to speak into each other's minds, but we weren't, so we'd have to make do with head gestures.

I nodded and walked over to the warm spot she'd been lying in, plopping down immediately.

When I saw that she was fully awake and walking around and wasn't likely to be surprised in an ambush, I closed my eyes and tried to push thoughts of fifteen-year-old Axil from my mind. I hadn't allowed myself to think about him so deeply in years. Going back to those memories hurt, and I realized that not getting closure, not being able to tell him how he hurt me was what killed me. I'd felt bound and gagged, unable to share my side of it. Sleep pulled at my limbs and I pushed Axil from my mind but those piercing blue eyes kept coming back to me.

My future wife.

Did he have any idea that I would actually be in the running one day for such a thing? No. How could he? With a deep sigh, I lowered my head and then I was out.

The sound of deep growling pulled me from my slumber. I was so tired. I couldn't have been asleep more than an hour given how groggy my body felt. I blinked rapidly, popping up onto all four paws and looked around.

Oh no.

Eliza's hackles were up as she crouched in front of me and faced the oncoming pack of wolven. Four of them.

It must be Ivanna and her new crew. I was suddenly overly alert, blood pumping through my veins as all sleepiness fled from my system. I stepped forward, next to Eliza and peered over at her.

She looked scared and I knew why. Fighting a pack of four wolves when you couldn't communicate was a death sentence.

If only she were pack.

A wild idea hit me then and before I had time to overthink it, I lunged forward and bit into her hind leg lightly, just enough to draw blood.

She yelped and tried to jerk away from me.

'I claim you, Eliza Green, for Mud Flat pack,' I said in my mind and then released her, biting my own leg next. The second our blood mixed in my mouth, I pulled up every ounce of dominant power I possessed. I wasn't an alpha, but I could be one day if I wanted to. Dorian was training me as such and he'd shown me how to claim a wolf. Normally it was a power only an alpha or second in command possessed but I was hoping that I had enough magic to pull this off and that Dorian wouldn't mind me doing so.

A blue dusting of light fell over my fur, flickering like fireflies, and then Eliza looked up at me wide-eyed.

'Did you just claim me?' she shrieked into my mind.

It worked!

'Yes. Incoming.' I barely had time to communicate before the wolves were upon us. They spread out in a circle, surrounding us and now that they were closer, I could smell which one Ivanna was. A medium-sized black and gray wolf.

'We attack together. Taking each one down separately, that will hopefully frighten the others off,' I told her.

'Okay.' Her voice was shaky, even in my head.

I didn't want to take Ivanna down first because the other three would jump in to protect her, as she was the most dominant. Instead, I aimed for the smallest one to Eliza's left.

'Her.'

I lowered my head and growled low as they circled, trying to intimidate us.

Without another word Eliza lunged forward and yanked the small wolf by the hind leg, dragging her into the circle. The other three wolves lunged for Eliza but I got into the fray first. While Eliza was dragging in the small wolf, who howled in pain and tried to claw at the ground and run out, I went for her jugular.

I bit down on her throat and tore it out in seconds as her body went limp. She didn't even know what hit her. It was the same tactic that my pack used to take down cougarin.

Suddenly a wolf landed on my back. I shook vigorously to dislodge her before she could bite me and felt her slide off.

'Help!' Eliza called and I spun to see Ivana tearing into her flank. Eliza kept her head low to the ground with her throat covered by the dirt as one of the other wolves tugged at her ear, trying to get her to expose her neck.

I leapt into the air and came down on Ivanna's back hard, knocking her to the side. She rolled three times, out of the way.

'*Attack!*' I told Eliza and without hesitation she stood from where she was protectively cowering and we both went for the wolf who'd been pulling on her ear. This time I pulled her hind leg to pin her down and Eliza tore out her throat. It all happened in a matter of seconds. There was nothing compared to fighting with a packmate. Not only could we verbally communicate but I sensed things. Her flank was hurting and she was hungry but she was also roaring with fighting energy and there was a trust between us.

She would do as I asked, letting me take the lead.

We both turned then, just as Ivanna and her final wolf stepped before us, lips peeled back in a snarl. Ivanna looked at the two dead wolves and then at the both of us.

She knew. She knew we were pack. It was the only way we could pull off such a coordinated attack.

She took two steps back, then three, and was halfway out of the fighting ring before her loner wolf friend realized what was happening.

They were going to retreat.

Part of me wanted to take them both out now. Together, as a pack, we probably could, but Eliza was injured, I could sense it.

'*How badly are you hurt?*' I asked her.

'*Who cares. Let's finish them.*'

I turned and gave her a wolfish grin. I knew I'd originally liked her for a reason. But when I saw the hunk of fur and flesh hanging off her ribcage and the pool of blood beneath her, fear washed over me.

Ivanna and her wolf used my distraction then to tuck tail and run, heading for the open flat landscape around us.

Knowing they were gone and wouldn't likely come back, I ran to Eliza and used my nose to bring the flap of fur up to her exposed ribcage.

She whimpered.

'*Lie down,*' I commanded.

She plopped down in her own blood and I used my nose to stick the skin back to her flank so that it could heal properly.

She needed food. Raw meat preferably.

I peered at the two dead wolves laying around us and Eliza looked up at me.

'*I'm not that hungry,*' she assured me.

'*I didn't say anything.*' I tried to act innocent.

'*You were thinking it.*'

Damn, she already knew me too well. I'd never eaten my own kind, couldn't even fathom it until now.

'*I'll be fine with some rest and water,*' she said.

I moved to grab one of the water bead strings and then dragged it over to her. She crushed the bulbs in her mouth and then began to pant.

Panting meant pain and I was about to make things worse because my instinct was telling me that lying injured near two fresh kills was a stupid idea. *'We should move. These bodies are going to attract animals.'*

I hated myself for saying it because I knew she would do as I asked. With a wide-eyed look of horror, she nodded once and tried to stand. She fell twice and I felt awful.

'I can shift and carry you,' I said.

'Don't you dare,' she snapped. *'Save your energy, they could come back and we still have to walk out of here.'*

On her third attempt, I used my snout to help her stand and she stumbled forward, out of the blood puddle and away from the carnage.

'Even a quarter of a mile will help us. Anything to put a distance between us and the bodies,' I told her.

She limped, whimpering with each step as we moved away from where the fight had gone down. When we'd gotten a good enough way away, I called for her to stop. She did, and promptly fell to the ground with a yelp.

I immediately nuzzled her neck, fear gripping me. I felt so conflicted. She was now my packmate, someone I had a connection with. I could *feel* her pain. I couldn't just let her die. She was more injured than she'd let on. I saw that now. Blood pooled around her and I knew that without food, her healing magic would be slow. Too slow.

'I'm sorry I couldn't protect you,' I told her. The fact that we were both in a competition to win the Queen

Trials didn't matter anymore. Only this bond mattered, she was a pack sister now.

Cyrus was going to kill me because I knew in this moment I could never hurt her. If we both made it back to Death Mountain alive and I was put in a fight against her, I couldn't do it.

What had I done?

She looked up at me. *'If I'm not better tomorrow morning, leave me.'*

I growled, as if that was a crazy thing to say. *'Pack-mates stick together,'* I told her.

She shook her head. *'I don't want Ivanna marrying the king and leading my people. Leave me and win the trials.'*

A whimper lodged in my throat then and I fell onto the ground next to her, snuggling up to her good side.

'Tell me a story,' she said. *'Distraction helps with the pain and hunger.'*

And so I did. I told her my secret, one very few people knew.

'I knew King Axil before when he was just a young teenager. I loved him.'

She gasped, a small wolfish sound and I nodded, proceeding to tell her the entire story. Why not? She might bleed out right here in the middle of nowhere and I wanted to share the weight of what I carried with someone else. She listened quietly and then I finished with him walking away with his brother after King Ansel had said all of those horrible things about me.

'*That explains so much,*' she said sleepily when I finished.

I frowned. '*What do you mean?*'

She stared at me, her yellow wolf eyes searing into my soul. '*My sister works in the palace as Axil's personal assistant. She once questioned why he never took lovers.*'

My heart frantically pounded against the walls of my chest. '*What did he say?*'

'*That he'd already given his heart away when he was fifteen and anything else would pale in comparison,*' Eliza replied blearily.

My muzzle unhinged as her words hit me like tossed stones. He ... he said that about *me*? It didn't make sense, he was the one who walked away.

When I glanced back down at Eliza, her eyes were closed, and she was asleep.

I didn't say anything more, my stomach was tied into knots over Eliza's state of health and I was still processing her words about Axil. She must be mistaken, heard her sister wrong. Axil wouldn't say that about me ... I shook myself, pushing all of that away.

Even though I knew we should be moving and making as much distance between the two dead wolven bodies as possible, I forced myself to keep watch as Eliza slept. She needed the healing rest more than anything.

A few hours ticked by and I constantly had to make myself get up and move in circles to keep awake. I was just making the hundredth circle around Eliza when I smelled it.

I froze, my wolf snout tipping up into the air so that I could take in a deep breath.

No.

Bearin.

It must have found the two dead wolves. We had to get out of here. Eliza was covered in blood and he would find her too and finish us both off. I'd fought bearin plenty of times with my pack, but never alone. Lone wolves got picked off by bearin.

"*Liza.*' I nudged her with my snout, shortening her name in a rush.

When her head lolled to the side, limp, I whimpered.

No.

Pressing my nose tightly to her neck, I nearly cried in relief when I felt a strong pulse. She was passed out, which wasn't good, but she also wasn't dead.

I would have to shift into my human form and carry her, not stopping until we reached Death Mountain. She was family. Pack. As much as Cyrus would have counseled me to leave her behind, I couldn't now. I'd bonded myself to this woman and I wasn't going to let her die.

Dammit, Zara.

I was just about to force myself to change when I heard heavy footsteps behind me.

No. No. No.

I was too late.

Spinning around, I came face to face with the black bearin. The only saving grace was that he was smaller, a younger male who was still nearly twice my size but nothing like the adult males who were four times my wolf.

Every instinct inside of me urged me to run but then I remembered the way Eliza had stood over me when I was waking up from whatever they'd drugged us with. She'd protected me when Ivanna tried to take me out. She was loyal and I wasn't going to lose my honor by leaving a packmate behind. I'd rather die here protecting her body than run back to Death Mountain a coward and a pack traitor.

When the bearin reared up on his hind legs and snarled, I lowered into an attack stance and let out a deep growl. I could see blood stains on his mouth where he'd already dug into our earlier kills but clearly he wasn't satiated. I needed to let him know that if he messed with me, it meant he would be injured. Then maybe I could get him to run off.

He charged then, and instead of thinking up some cool plan, I was thrown into the fight of my life running on instinct.

He was larger and slower. When he lunged for me, I leapt up into the air, planning to come down on top of him.

He was smarter than that unfortunately. Reaching up with his giant paw, he batted me out of the sky like a ball.

My ribs snapped on impact with his paw and then I

went flying. I braced myself for the hit and when my body crashed into the hard ground I wailed in pain. My already broken ribs flared to life with agony upon impact. A fresh wave of anguish took my breath away but I got up quickly. I expected the beast to come for me again but to my horror, he was going for bloody and unconscious Eliza.

I might be able to use this to my benefit. Sprinting from where I had fallen, I took off after the animal before he could get to Eliza, who was just lying there, limp and helpless. I leapt on the bearin's back, tearing into the side of his neck. The second I got a good bite in, he stood erect, shaking me off. I fell, landing on those cracked ribs again and nearly passed out from the searing hot wave of agony. I had to remind myself that pain was temporary and to just push past it. Nothing mattered more than staying alive right now. The bearin had realized that I was the biggest threat in the area and officially charged me head-on. This little bastard had pissed me off and I went absolutely berserk on him. I always knew I would die in battle. Or hoped I would. It was the ultimate honor. And dying while tearing into this pain in my ass, protecting a new friend and packmate, was a fine way to go for me.

I snapped at him like a rabid animal, tearing into flesh and ripping away hunks of his fur as his jaws came around my leg and chomped.

A howl of misery ripped from my throat but I didn't let up, making sure that this coward would be scarred for life before I died. When I clamped down on his back leg and heard the rewarding crunch of bone, he released me all at once and stumbled backwards with a limp.

I held my injured back leg up in the air so as not to put any pressure on it and stared him down. He was doing the same, favoring his other paws while curling the one I'd maimed up to his belly.

We were in an epic stare-down.

I can do this all day. I will fight you to the death, you piece of crap, and take your eyeball on my way to Hades.

On instinct I snarled and lunged for him, hopping on my good back leg and he turned and ran off.

Relief rushed through me as I watched him go, but I held firm, staying standing as I watched him become a small dot on the horizon. The sun was up now and we needed to get out of here before more predators came.

A moan came from behind me and I hopped over to Eliza. She was conscious but when I placed my muzzle against hers, I felt the fever through her fur.

Infection.

The bleeding had stopped thanks to her healing abilities but she needed food and rest to fight the infection.

I knew what I had to do.

Forcing a shift with broken bones was liable to give you a permanent injury. You should always wait until the bones had set but I didn't have time for that. Eliza would die without getting back to Death Mountain and so would I. It was the worst pain in my life.

I wished I'd had the energy to kill the bearin because it

would have given us sustenance but I was grateful to have scared it off. Whimpering and howling through the searing pain of my shift, I finally stood on one leg, naked as the day I was born. I was too terrified to put pressure on my other foot just yet. I'd long forgotten about our clothing back at the site of the fight and was going to have to get over the fact that I was gonna walk over twelve hours back into Death Mountain nude. Nudity wasn't a big deal among our people, a breast here, a flash of backside there. We all shifted back and forth between our forms regularly but to walk into a crowd of clothed humans while fully naked ...

I shook my head, not caring about something so trivial. Reaching down to hook the water bulb vines around my neck, I hopped over to Eliza and hefted her over my shoulders like I would a kill, still not putting pressure on my broken foot.

'No,' she said weakly into my mind. '*Leave me and save yourself.*'

'*Not a chance in Hades,*' I told her and winced at the discomfort her weight put on my healing broken ribs.

She didn't argue, I believed she was too weak and now that she was draped over my shoulders like a furry scarf, I could feel that she was burning up. Way too hot.

I had yet to take the first step. I was scared of what it would feel like to carry my own weight, plus Eliza's, on a broken ankle that wasn't fully set but I knew I had to move or die.

I took one step and then stumbled forward with a cry. It was so much worse than I thought; hot pain like fire licked up my ankle and caused sweat to bead my brow.

'*Pain is temporary. Work around it.*' Cyrus' voice came to me then. It was as if he could feel my distress all the way from his place on Death Mountain and was trying to counsel me.

I looked around frantically and nearly wept with relief when I saw a long sturdy branch that I could use as a walking stick. Hoping over to it, while keeping Eliza on my shoulders, took talent but when I got there, I bent down to pick it up. It was thick, not completely straight but straight enough. Ripping the extra branches from it, I fisted the tip of it and stuck the blunt end into the ground, walking forward cautiously.

It still hurt, but it took enough weight off my ankle that the pain was bearable. Though I had to keep Eliza balanced on my shoulders with just one hand, I was managing. The flat landscape was forgiving. I was thankful I didn't have to jump over any fallen logs or giant rocks but after the second hour I started to go slightly insane.

Eliza was hot and heavy, my ribs seemed to be healing but now my stomach was eating itself inside out, begging for food. As a shifter I burned more calories than a human on a normal day, but an injured shifter could eat enough food for twenty humans.

My foot was a constant throb and sometimes a sharp stab if I moved too quickly.

By the fourth hour I wanted to die. Eliza had passed out again, her head flopping against my neck. I reached a few dark minutes where I considered leaving her. It would be much easier to walk without the giant wolf around my shoulders.

Pain is temporary, I told myself.

Except when it's not. When it's going on for several hours of pain and hunger, it felt *very* permanent.

I started to sing then. Lightly, so I wouldn't waste energy but I had to do something or I would go completely mad.

"When the little baby wolf went over the ridge, over the ridge ..." I smiled as I was reminded of my baby brother Oslo and the songs I would sing him to sleep with, *"... he found his mama wolf in the meadow."* I finished and was shocked when a tear slipped down my cheek and into Eliza's fur.

I had officially cracked.

I never cried. Tears were for weak submissives who needed protection. Not me. Not Zara Swiftwater, daughter of an alpha.

Reaching up, I smacked myself across the cheek and shook my head.

Get it together, Zara.

Only by pulling on every ounce of my strength was I going to survive this. Now was not the time to go soft.

Somehow, I walked for another six hours, taking as few breaks as possible, until I felt dead inside and out.

I stared up at the sun, making sure for the hundredth time I was going south and then looked out on the horizon.

A sob left my throat when I saw the back side of Death Mountain come into view. It was far off in the distance, but it was there.

We made it.

"Almost there. Hang on, 'Liza," I told her and pushed forward with a renewed strength.

By my estimate it took another two hours to finally reach the base of the mountain. I'd been walking for over twelve hours, the sun was setting in the sky and I was dead on my feet but somehow I kept going. The broken barren land turned to lush forest abruptly and pretty soon I was having to amble over fallen trees and sharp inclines.

Everything hurt. It burned, it throbbed, it pounded like a heartbeat in my foot but not more than my desire to get us both to safety, to food and rest.

Climbing up the back of that mountain tested my soul to its very limits. I fell twice. Dropped Eliza once. I cried, I screamed, I howled and finally when I came up over the ridge ... I'd made it. I was covered in blood and dirt and my foot was black and purple and bent at an odd angle. Eliza looked half-dead, she smelled rotten, and she was center of the sun hot, but I could still hear her heartbeat.

The noises of the people of Death Mountain pulled at my ears and I followed the sound, all but dragging myself through the thick woods and into the open grassy knoll at the base of the castle.

People stared as I limped forward, naked and barely alive, towards the blue champion tent and then all at once there was shouting.

"Champions are back!"

"Get her water!"

"Medical!" one lady screamed as she frantically took in my distressed state and started to rush forward.

I couldn't hold on any longer; at the sight of safety my strength had fled. The crowd parted and then Axil jogged forward with wide panicked eyes, taking me in from head to toe. I stumbled, swaying on my feet.

The woman who had called for help took Eliza off my shoulders and I tried to stay upright but my legs suddenly felt like they were made of liquid with no substance to keep them standing.

One second I was looking at Axil's terrified gaze and the next I was falling. His arms crashed around me and then I was enveloped with his scent.

Maker, I missed that smell. I missed the way I felt tucked against his muscular chest.

"She brought in another wolf!" someone commented.

"Why would she do that? She could have left her?" another said as they attended to Eliza and my vision started to blur.

Axil reached out and traced my jaw like he had a

hundred times, all while holding my gaze. "Because that's Zara. She's loyal."

He said it like he knew my soul inside and out and to be seen like that, it made a part of me come alive again. A part I thought had died.

And that's when everything went black and I lost my battle with staying conscious.

I came to with the sound of arguing voices.

"Eliza says she's pack with her!" an older male shouted.

"That's against the rules. Only one wolf per pack may enter the Queen Trials," another man said.

It sounded like the elder advisors were arguing. My body was still sore and I wanted to hear what they were saying so I continued to lie there quietly with my eyes pinched shut.

"*I'm* the king," Axil growled. "And I say it's not. Both women entered the trials from different packs. We told them to survive the task and they did what they had to in order to do that."

"But—" one went to argue then stopped, probably getting a glare from Axil.

"They would have an extreme advantage in the next task, my lord," the more reasonable voice added.

"Then so be it. You want me to marry the strongest member of our kind. Well, I think a woman *who isn't even an alpha*, and was able to force a pack bond, is pretty damn strong," Axil said and my belly warmed.

• He was talking about me.

There was the sound of shuffling feet then as they retreated from the room and my eyelids sprang open. I was in an elvin crystal healing chamber bed with stark white sheets draped over my body. I realized then that not everyone had left, and I peered up to find Axil looking down at me.

"How's—" I started but he waved me off.

"She's fine. You saved her life." His words were clipped and short.

Why did he sound upset? I propped myself up onto my elbows. "And you're mad about that?" I growled. "You haven't changed a bit. Still the same selfish little boy who only cares about his royal reputation!"

I didn't care that he was king now, Axil Moon needed to be taken down a notch. He didn't have a right to be angry at me for saving someone's life.

At my words, he recoiled as if I'd slapped him. "Is that what you think?"

All the pain I swore I'd gotten over as a young teen came flooding to the surface. "Yes, Axil. Did you black out at our break-up? Your brother informed you that I was a piece of Mud Flat trash and you agreed and walked away. Never even came back the next year. Never sent a letter. *Nothing*."

His cheeks burned with shame, redness washing over his neck. "I didn't agree." His voice was small and he looked horrified, eyes wide as he began to fidget with his hands.

I laughed, a biting sound. "The silence and sight of your back as you walked away was agreement enough."

He frowned. "You hate me. I've spent all of these years loving you and you *hate* me?" He sounded surprised.

His words were like an arrow to my heart. I sat up fully now, pleased to feel no pain in my ribs, just the aching in my soul at his words. I was clothed, even if it was in a white healing gown, and so I slipped off the bed and hobbled towards him, testing the weight on my ankle. It was tender but nothing like before. It made me wonder how long I'd been out, but I no longer cared in this moment.

"Loving me?" Instead of feeling joy, I had never been more pissed off in my life. "You think that walking away after those two months at camp—"

"I—"

"DO NOT INTERUPT ME!" I shouted like a crazed maniac, pulling dominant power into my voice and his eyes flew wide. "I've waited five years to tell you this, Axil Moon, you will let me speak my truth!"

Axil looked scared of me and deep down that made me feel good. I wanted him to hurt. I shuffled closer to him so that I could look him straight in the eyes as I told him what he did to me. He appeared like he was in pain before I even opened my mouth.

With a shaky breath, I held his gaze. "I'm dead inside because of you, Axil."

Agony crossed his face and he stumbled backwards into the wall until his back hit it. I pushed forward, stepping closer so that I could reach out and touch his heart with my hand. I laid my palm over the spot on his chest that contained his heart, like I had so many times that summer. Feeling the frantic chaotic beating made me feel good.

"I loved you with every ounce of my soul, the entire weight of it was yours," I told him. "You made promises, knowing how broken I was from losing my parents so young. You told me that *you* would be my family," I reminded him.

Shame burned his cheeks but he stayed silent, letting me speak my truth.

"And then you left me. Threw me away like trash!" I

screamed in his face, retracting my hand. "And now every man that has come after you has gotten a shadow of me because there's nothing left!" I beat on my chest hard, as my wolf rose to the surface and Axil did something I didn't expect.

He covered his face with his hands and burst into sobs.

The raw heartfelt emotion shook me to my core and I didn't know what to do with it. Axil Moon, the *king wolven,* didn't cry. He wasn't weak. He didn't break down in sobs over a woman.

Or did he? And was it a weakness?

I stared at him in shock as he broke down and part of me wanted to pull him into my arms and squeeze him so tight until he stopped, but the bigger part wanted him to hurt. So I turned, and hopped out of the room, slamming the door and leaving my past behind me.

Hurt me once. Lesson learned. Hurt me twice ... never gonna happen, because I'm not that stupid.

Axil Moon was dead to me.

I RUSHED RIGHT OUTSIDE, through the network of hallways and found my brother.

He started to lay into me about making Eliza pack but when he saw the look on my face he stopped. He handed me a large piece of flatbread with butter on it and my mouth instantly watered. I yanked it from his grasp and then slipped past him and into my hammock without saying another word. I wanted to be alone, just me and my yummy flatbread and my stupid feelings. Sometime later I fell asleep and then woke up early the next morning. The campfire was dying and the sun was barely out.

I stepped out of the tent to find that my ankle could now support all of my weight.

Cyrus didn't look up at me as he added another log to the fire. "Ivanna and one other made it back late last night. They looked half-starved but not severely injured."

I nodded, handing him a second log without speaking. I knew Ivanna would survive but I didn't care right now. I hadn't been able to get Axil's words out of my head all night.

I've spent all these years loving you and you hate me?

Did he really believe he loved me all these years? The sound of his sobbing haunted my soul. Maybe he did.

I'd never seen a man break down like that. Hades, none of the women I knew cried like that. Unless they were submissive or had just lost a relative in battle. He cried like I'd died. Maybe I'd mourned him all those years ago and for some stupid reason he'd held on to hope? So he'd only just lost me last night.

It didn't make sense.

I didn't see how he could be so delusional but alas, men were stupid sometimes.

My brother finally spoke. "You made her pack? Zara, are you insane?"

Eliza. I needed to check on her. "Maybe," I told him and he finally looked up at me with a little compassion.

"You okay? Was it rough out there?"

I sighed, "If killing two wolves, while fighting off another two, and then being mauled by a bearin, only to walk Eliza out on a broken ankle is rough ... then yeah it was."

He stood then, shifting on the balls of his feet before pulling me into an awkward stiff hug.

My brother didn't hug. Clearly. He was horrible at it. It actually hurt, he was squeezing my back so hard, but I said nothing. It would probably be another ten years before he hugged me again so I wrapped my arms around him and squeezed him back.

"I was so damn proud of you when you stepped out of those woods, Zar," he said, pulling back. "Mom and Dad would have been too."

Did his eyes look wet?

"Are you crying?" I teased him. Something was in the air. All these men crying over me.

"No!" he snapped, wiping at his eyes and then punching my shoulder hard for good measure.

I grinned. "I had help. Eliza kept me safe. We have an alliance."

His face fell. "That will only work until the final

round and then, if she's still alive, you're going to have to kill her."

My body physically clenched at the thought. "Cyrus, she's pack. I claimed her."

His fists clenched. "I know. I can *feel* her," he argued. "We all can." He gestured to my packmates who were stepping out of the tent and yawning with sleep.

They nodded.

Of course they could, she was family now. Mud Flat pack.

I shrugged. "I owe her my life. She stood over me and protected me when I was unconscious as Ivanna came for me with a sharp rock."

Cyrus looked disappointed. "Zara, two people can't win this."

"I know that!" I snapped. I didn't want to talk about this, I didn't want to think about killing my new friend and pack-mate. I couldn't hear this anymore. "Let's just focus on taking out Ivanna. That bitch has it in for me and I want her gone."

Cyrus nodded and then I told him I was going to get some fresh air and food. The piece of flatbread I'd had last night wasn't cutting it.

I knew that Eliza wouldn't sleep outside in tents so I walked to the castle and when the guard at the front saw me, he bowed deeply.

"Zara Swiftwater. It's an honor," he said.

I froze. He knew my name? "Uh thanks."

He seemed to read my shocked expression. "Eliza is Death Mountain pack. You didn't have to bring her home on your shoulders like that. You have all of our respect."

I smiled. "Yes, I did. She saved my life. Speaking of which, do you know which room is hers?"

He gestured down a long hallway. "Make a left and then it's the last one on the right."

I entered the stone castle and walked down the lengthy corridor, making a left at the fork until I came to the last door. Reaching out, I rapped my knuckles on the door he'd spoken of. I sensed her. She was inside full of nervous energy. The door opened and then she stood before me with a bandaged ribcage and wearing a cropped top. There were black circles under her eyes and she smelled of raw meat but she was alive. We both took one look at each other and then rushed into the other's arms. I held her gently, knowing she was still injured, and she did the same.

"Thank you," she said, her voice thick with emotion. "You saved my life."

I pulled back from her. "You saved mine first. Ivanna would have bashed my head open with that rock."

She smiled, waving me into the room.

I stepped inside, taking in the luxurious digs. "Wait, why did I say no to this in order to sleep in a tent?" I asked.

She laughed. "I have no idea."

It wasn't a room, it was a house! Or as big as one anyway. There was a large great room with a small kitchen and what looked like two bedrooms. The floors were a rich brown-stained wood and the walls were painted a light yellow.

My joke had lightened the mood but I could tell by the look on her face, she was about to say something that would bring me back down.

"You'll make an amazing queen," she told me and I froze.

"Stop it," I said.

She shook her head. "Zara, how do you think this ends? I just heard the next round is paired fighting. You and me against Ivanna and Charlize. The winning team then fights each other."

I gasped. I didn't know that. Did Cyrus? Maybe that's what he was trying to say at the fire.

"I ... can't kill you, Eliza. I'm a lot of things but I'm not capable of that." I was surprised to find that it was true. I thought myself tougher than that, especially considering I'd known this girl only a few days but there was something about her. A sisterly bond I couldn't explain.

She shrugged. "You kill me or I forfeit and my pack tears me apart. Your choice."

"Stop it!" I shouted. "Let's not even talk about that. We could die in the next challenge."

Eliza shook her head, her blonde curls spilling around her. "You know we won't. We have a pack advantage. You lead, I'll follow."

My heart pinched at her loyalty to me. "We shouldn't

have become friends," I said, feeling bad once the words left my mouth. I didn't really mean it but I kind of did. It would have been easier that way. Somewhere in the last three near-death experiences I'd had with this woman, we'd forged an unbreakable bond. "I didn't mean that," I said.

She reached over and placed her hand on mine. "I know what you meant."

"Axil said he still loved me," I blurted out, changing the subject, not used to having a girlfriend to talk to, having grown up with two brothers.

She gasped and stepped closer to me, full-on grinning. "And?"

"I told him off. And then he sobbed."

Her eyebrows shot up. "King Axil *sobbed?*"

I nodded.

"Damn, what did you say to him?" She looked concerned and now I wondered if I'd gone too far in some of the things I'd said to him.

"Just the usual post break-up stuff, that I was dead inside now, that he broke my heart and I was a shadow of my former self," I teased.

She burst into laughter and then grabbed her bandaged side, wincing.

"You okay?" I asked, hoping she would be healthy enough for our doubles fight.

She nodded. "Still healing. Have you eaten?"

The moment she said it, my stomach came to life.

That flatbread wasn't enough and I'd been half conscious when I'd eaten it. Now I smelled the meat in her kitchen and my stomach growled loudly.

"Feed me immediately," I ordered with a mock seriousness.

With a smile she walked gingerly over to the kitchen and pulled out a plate of various smoked meats, bread rolls and cheeses. I dug in without even waiting to be offered. Like a crazed lunatic I shoved meat and cheese into my mouth, half chewing before swallowing it down. It was spicy and salty and so, so good.

Eliza looked at me horrified. "I take it back, you would make a horrible queen, you have no manners."

I gave her my middle finger and she grinned.

We got along so easily, it was like the best friend I never had in the Mud Flats. Every female there was either competing to be the most dominant, and therefore steering clear of each other, or they were so submissive they barely spoke to me. With Eliza, it was an easy friendship, she knew her pecking order in the pack was beneath me but she was dominant enough to give me crap, which I appreciated.

"Could you drop out?" I asked her. "You're injured."

She laughed. "You think they care about an injury? A drop-out is the same as forfeit. I'll be killed and seen as bringing shame to the whole pack. The *king's* pack."

I lost my appetite then, feeling sick thinking about the possibility of eventually having to fight Eliza.

"Thanks for the food. I should probably go." I suddenly didn't want to be here, bonding with her only to be pitted against each other another day.

She looked sad but nodded, handing me a glass of water to wash all the food down. I drank it and thanked her, leaving out the door to her apartment.

As I walked the halls of the castle I couldn't stop thinking about Eliza. *Stupid Zara. I should have told her to pound sand the first day I met her.* I never should have helped her win her fights or given her advice. And I *never* should have made her pack. Now I was stuck with her. The best part about the Queen Trials was that there was only one person per pack and you didn't know any of them. It was easier to kill people you didn't know. Like Ivanna.

I was so stuck in my head that I realized I was now lost. I'd gone the wrong way and turned to retrace my steps when I slammed into someone's chest.

Axil.

My whole body froze.

He looked down at me and after yesterday's emotional exchange I wasn't prepared to see the mask of anger that was displayed there.

I sucked in a breath at the sight and he gritted his jaw and moved to walk past me. I stepped to the side, matching his movements but getting in his way. His nostrils flared and pure unbridled rage roiled through him. I could *feel* it.

How dare he.

"You have *no* right to be mad at me," I seethed, holding his dominant gaze.

"You didn't even let me speak," he managed through clenched teeth.

I scoffed. "And what could you possibly say that would explain how you just walked away from me? After all the promises you made."

He looked farther down the hallway where footsteps could be heard and then reached out, yanking me by the shoulders and pulling me into an open doorway.

I growled but allowed him to shuffle me into a room and shut the door. I peered around to see that we were in some kind of library. Books lined dark wooden floor-to-ceiling bookshelves.

He rushed forward then, zooming into my face with as much anger as I'd had during our last exchange. Dark circles marred his skin and I wondered if he'd slept last night. "You're not serious about me walking away, right? You had to have known that it was against my will."

I scoffed, looking at him like he'd grown two heads. "Against your will? The second your brother showed up and started to call me trash, you shut down and walked away without a fight ..."

As soon as I said it out loud, it hit me. Why in Hades had I never thought of it before? His brother was king at the time and therefore had the gift that every wolven king had ...

"He controlled you." I said it with complete shock, feeling badly for how I'd treated him, thinking for all those years that he'd walked away willingly.

"Yes," he said through gritted teeth, "and never permitted me to return to the summer camp. I can't *believe* you would think that I left you like that."

My heart hammered in my chest at his words, and some part of me, deep down inside, healed. He didn't leave me. He was *taken* away from me. There was a difference.

Axil leaned his forehead against mine, like he used to when we were kids. "How could you ever think I'd willingly spend even one day away from you?"

I whimpered then, feeling my own breakdown just beneath the surface.

"My lord!" someone shouted in the hallway, the sound muffled by the closed door.

Axil growled and stepped away from me. I spun,

giving him my back just as the door opened. I had to bite my lip to keep from falling into a fit of sobs right there.

"I have an urgent matter that needs your attention, sir," a male voice said from outside.

Axil hesitated, probably looking at me and waiting for my reaction.

"I'll be out in a minute," Axil said.

"My lord, it's extremely urgent," the guard pressed. "We have news of war."

My wolf bristled at that.

War?

Axil reached for me, grasping my shoulders. "Let's talk later. I'm not done with you."

I'm not done with you. There was more. Of course there was. There was five years of absence to explain.

Footsteps fell away from me and then the door shut. I couldn't hold it in any longer. Collapsing to the ground I burst into cries reminiscent of the night Axil left me. Fat hot tears fell down my cheeks as I relived what I'd said to him last night. How I'd squarely placed all the blame on him.

He was taken. Forced to leave. It made sense, how he'd shut down as soon as his brother caught us lying together in the grass and kissing. He had been so emotionless I thought he was embarrassed to be found with me, but now I knew he was under the control of the king. A power that Axil now carried in his veins, to render any one of the wolven under his complete control, like a puppet.

That's what Ansel did to him.

This was all too much to process so quickly. Axil had pined for me this entire time and was held against his will from seeing me?

It was crazy. Surely not for five years?

I cried so hard then. I cried for all the years I'd blamed him, for all the kisses that were stolen from us. The shock of this new information seeped deeply into the very core of my being.

He didn't leave. But staying away for five years? He'd been king for two. Why not come for me then? I had so many questions but I was too overwhelmed to deal with them. Sucking back my tears, I wiped at my eyes and stood, forcing myself to get it together.

I was going into a doubles fight soon, I needed to stay strong.

No matter what happened with Axil and I when we were kids, it didn't change the fact that we were different people now. I wasn't that same love-drunk young wolf he fell for. Life had hardened me, and so had our break-up, whether he intended it to or not.

Taking a steadying breath, I left the library and found my way back to the tents outside. Cyrus was waiting for me and we ran over some drills as I threw myself into my training, pushing everything I'd just learned deep down inside of me.

I couldn't deal with it right now; it would make me emotional and emotions made you weak. I'd learned that the advisors had agreed to pair Eliza and me up against Ivanna and Charlize and that the fight was tomorrow morning, and so Eliza came by with her coach and we trained together in wolf form first, then in human.

"They're good together," I overheard Cyrus telling Eliza's coach.

"That would be the pack bond," Jonas, her coach, said with a bit of disdain in his voice.

I couldn't imagine anyone from Death Mountain pack was happy I'd altered the pack bonds and basically stolen Eliza.

"Mmm," Cyrus just grunted, about as excited that Eliza and I now shared a pack bond as Jonas was.

I wondered if Axil was allowing us to keep the bond for the doubles fight and would take Eliza back into Death Mountain pack once we'd won.

We *were* winning. I would accept nothing less.

The more the night pressed on, the more I thought about Axil. What war news had he been taken away to talk about? We hadn't gone to war in ages but I knew the other realms fought with the Nightfall queen often. Was she finally coming for us?

How could you ever think I'd willingly spend even one day away from you?

I'm not done with you.

Axil's words plagued me all night as I tried to sleep, until I ached to see him again, to finish what we started today. I needed answers. I needed closure. As I peered over the side of my hammock, I noticed Cyrus was fast asleep, his leg hanging out of his hammock limply.

I slowly slipped out of mine and padded across the tent barefoot until I got outside. Two of my packmates were chatting by the fire and I quickly thought up a lie when they peered over at me.

"Going to Eliza's to talk strategy for tomorrow," I told them.

Not that they would care where I was going or try to stop me, but I didn't want anyone knowing Axil and I had a romantic involvement. As far as I knew, only Cyrus and Dorian knew about it because they'd been the ones to pick up the pieces when I fell apart after Axil left me discarded as trash.

But he didn't, I reminded myself. His stupid brother did and yet I needed more answers before I believed all that.

I made my way through the tents, across the front lawn and then right up to the front door of the palace. It was late and I was kind of hoping Axil would have come to see me but I realized he might either be busy doing kingly things, or not want to talk about all this stuff with me. But he *had* told me we would talk later and I wasn't going to be able to sleep tonight unless I knew why he didn't even send a note to me in five years.

I walked up to the guard and prepared a big speech, because it was forbidden to have any type of relationship during the trials. I didn't want him to know that I was here to see Axil. It was the same guard from before so I knew I didn't have to introduce myself.

I opened my mouth to speak when he beckoned me closer. "Are you here to see the king?" he whispered discreetly. There were still some wolves walking around the courtyard. People had been partying each night of the Queen Trials and I knew if word got around that Axil and I were once an item ... it could get me in major trouble.

My cheeks burned red but I nodded once.

Without further interrogation he left his station and turned inside, walking down a hallway I hadn't used earlier in the day.

I followed him as he made twists and turns until finally we reached another door with a different guard.

That new guard took one look at me and opened the door to a room, gesturing that I enter. "The king said that if you came looking for him, you were to wait in here," the new guard said. "He is finishing up a meeting."

He did? My stomach dropped when I thought of how thoughtful that was. And clearly his men weren't going to tell the advisors I was here. "Thank you." I dipped my chin and then entered the room, leaving both guards behind me. They shut the door and it was in that moment that I realized I was in Axil's private living quarters. The space opened into a giant sitting room with a dark red velvet sofa and a roaring fire. I inhaled and had to suppress a moan. It smelled like him. *Like pine trees and moss, and man.* Stepping farther into the room, I peered to the right, through the open double doors and my gaze landed on a giant bed with red silk sheets and a cream fur blanket.

Axil's favorite color had always been red.

My mind then went to how many women had seen this bed. According to Eliza's sister, not many. I had to fight the urge to riffle through every single drawer and cubby hole. I didn't know grown King Axil. I only knew the boy, the young prince who I wasn't even aware was royalty at the time.

Young Axil was an expert marksman. He was a future alpha, the most dominant man I ever met. He liked to hunt elkin and sing songs by the fire with his friends. He'd traced the freckles on my collarbone and told me how they reminded him of certain star patterns. I reached up and touched that spot now.

Older Axil was king. Still dominant. Still in love with the color red. But I knew nothing else about this man.

Seeing an open book on the sofa, I walked over and pick it up. Examining the leather tome, I stroked my fingers along the author's name. *A. Grey.*

Older Axil reads.

Just as I was about to flip the book open and see what it was about, the door opened behind me. I startled a little, clasping the book to my chest as my heart jumped.

Axil strode into the room, took one look at me and smiled. "Seeing you after the day I've had is about the best thing I can think of."

It was sweet, but I hadn't fully forgiven him yet, so I

ignored his comment. "What's the book about? A war manual?"

Wasn't that what all kings read about?

He chuckled. "No. It's a fantasy tale of a young woman who carries both light and dark magic. She reminds me of you."

My heart stopped beating then and I set the book down on the couch before standing tall again.

"Oh? What darkness do I carry?" I asked, crossing my arms over my chest in a protective gesture.

He looked regretful at saying that but stepped closer until he was only a few inches away from me. Just he and I standing in front of the fire. In his room. Adults. *Alone.*

"Well, when we were fifteen it was the loss of your parents." He reached out and stroked my cheek and it sent a zap of energy down my spine, causing me to swallow hard. "And now ... it's ..." His face fell. "My leaving you."

He was right about all of it. I did carry that darkness with me even to this day.

"Axil, I can believe your brother forced you magically to walk away from me that day ... but the day after? And the day after that? I'm sorry but I'm not stupid. I can't believe that."

He nodded and then reached down and grabbed the hem of his tunic. I stopped breathing when he started to pull it up over his head.

What the Hades was he—

A whimper lodged in my throat when I saw the

network of scars across his abdomen. I was forced to blink rapidly lest I fall into a puddle of tears. Reaching up, I traced a few of the thick jagged lines across his chest. "These weren't here before," I couldn't help but say. I'd stroked his bare chest under the moonlight many times. That summer we would shift from wolf form into human and put on the most basic of coverings. He was topless nearly the entire summer.

"I was imprisoned for two years after I walked away from you that day," he said, his voice growly and low.

Shock ripped through me. Was this common knowledge? Because I'd heard nothing of it. Two years?

"Why?"

"My brother had just become king and my instructors at the training camp said that I was perfect at everything and if he didn't watch out, I could overthrow him."

I placed my hand over my mouth in anticipation of what he would say next.

Axil looked pained then, like he didn't want to go back to that place in his memories and I wanted to tell him he didn't have to explain himself, but it would be a lie. I had to know. If I were ever going to trust him, I had to know everything.

"He beat me into submission every single day until he was sure I would never challenge him. I barely ate, he forced me to be scrawny and weak," Axil said and my wolf rose to the surface.

I wanted to hunt Ansel down right now and skin him

alive. I instinctively stepped closer. Without thinking, I threaded my fingers through Axil's, and his face relaxed.

"When he finally let me go, I had to play it safe. I didn't bulk up too much at first, didn't lead any hunts. I acted like a mid-pack dominant."

I nodded. It's what I would do. *Survive.*

"It was at that time, a few months after he let me out of chains, that I got a letter to you."

I frowned, shaking my head. "No letter ever got to me."

He sighed. "Dorian read it first. He sent it back to me."

My whole body broke out into chills. No. He wouldn't, not after hearing me cry myself to sleep for months. He was a good alpha, he wouldn't.

"No. I don't believe you." I dropped Axil's hand.

Axil nodded and then walked into the bedroom. I watched in horror as he went to a nightstand and opened a drawer.

No. As much as I wanted Axil to pull a note out of there, I also didn't want him to. Knowing Axil tried to reach me would heal something inside of me but knowing Dorian betrayed me would break me all over again.

Axil pulled a white folded note out and I suddenly felt sick. He walked towards me and I couldn't look away from all of the scars on his chest.

"He's a good alpha. A good alpha knows what's best for their wolf and I respected that," Axil said before giving me the note. "I wanted what was best for you too, for us," he whispered as our fingers touched while I was retrieving the note from him.

I growled at that; a good alpha didn't let me cry myself to sleep and think I was worthless trash. I had a feeling I was going to need to sit down for this. Dropping onto the sofa, I opened the note quickly and started to scan Axil's messy script.

> Zara,
> Where do I begin?
> Firstly, I hope you don't think I would ever just walk away from you like that. But I fear from the sobs I heard as I was forced to follow my brother home, that you did. My brother used his king's power over me, forcing my lips shut and my head down. When we got back to Death Mountain, he imprisoned me for two years.
> For seven hundred and thirty days I dreamt only of you.

I HAD to stop reading and cover my mouth as a sob erupted from my throat. Reading this letter in front of Axil was both rewarding and torture at the same time.

The sofa dipped and then Axil's firm hand was on my lower back, rubbing small circles there. I continued reading the last few lines.

You might not still want me, and that's okay, because I'm not ready to give you the life I promised you. I need some time to do that. But I wanted you to know I'm working on it and I promise one day I will send for you.
My mate.
My future wife.
I love you, Zara.
Now. Forever. Always.
Axil

I WHIMPERED, biting the inside of my cheeks to keep from crying. Then I flipped the note over, recognizing Dorian's handwriting immediately.

Axil,
You nearly broke her last time and it's been two years, she's finally over you. Don't write again unless it's to make her your wife.

Don't show up unless it's to offer courtship.
I'll tear you apart if I see you on my land
without a lifelong promise for that girl.
She's too good for you right now.

Dorian

I SMILED at Dorian's note and all the anger I thought I would feel for my alpha fled. At the two-year mark I was finally doing okay. I had started dating again and was no longer sulking and hating my life. Dorian was right, seeing this letter only to read that Axil could do nothing to be with me, would have sent me over the edge at the time.

"Can you believe he said that to me? That he would tear me apart? A prince in line to the throne!" Axil chuckled beside me.

I'd forgotten he was here. Setting the note on my lap, I folded and tucked it into my pocket. "I'm keeping it. It's mine," I declared.

He said nothing, only nodded.

"Why didn't you tell me you were a prince?"

He sighed. "Because I had no intention of taking the throne. I didn't want you to see me as someone I wasn't. I wanted nothing to do with this role. I wanted you, and a small house in a village somewhere with a dozen kids."

My heart pinched at that statement but I needed more information.

"Then why did you challenge Ansel for kingship? If you didn't want that life?"

He sighed, running his hands through his dark hair. "Two years in captivity gave me a lot of time to think. I never dreamed my brother would be capable of such cruelty. But knowing he could imprison me and control me for so long ... I knew I couldn't let him stay king. That you and I would never be safe."

I frowned. "I agree. But then why did you let your brother live? If he'd been controlling you against your will and you fought him for king and won – why let him keep his life?" I asked. I'd have killed him.

Axil's wolf surfaced then, eyes glowing yellow. "Wolven law states that two heirs of the royal bloodline must be alive at any given time. Ansel's wife was unable to give him a pup, so I had to let him live until I could marry and have children of my own."

Everything he said made sense but my heart still hurt for how things went down. "You've been king for two years ... you could have sent for me the day you were crowned." I fumbled for reasons not to forgive him.

"Could I have?" he asked. "Once I became king I realized the mistake I had made. A king must only take a wife through the Queen Trials. I'd trapped myself. Part of me wanted you to enter to become mine, and the other part wanted you to stay in the Mud Flats where you couldn't be hurt."

The wind knocked out of my lungs as he reached up and cupped my jaw in his hands. "You're my mate, Zara. I've known that since we were fifteen. Didn't you?"

Those damn tears that usually never surfaced were back and I blinked them away quickly. "I hoped," I said softly.

He looked at my face then, no doubt waiting for my verdict.

Was he forgiven?

My heart thundered in my chest as I weighed his words in the note, along with Dorian's response, and then finally Axil's invitation to beckon me for the Queen Trials. The first night he'd seen me at the registration dinner he'd said he regretted inviting me. It was because he feared I would be killed and he'd have to marry another. He did everything he'd said he would when we were fifteen. It just took longer than I thought it would.

I finally peered up at him. "You took too long," I told him.

His face fell, hands slipping away from me and he nodded, looking stricken.

I hadn't meant it like that, like it was too late.

Reaching out, I cupped his chin and drew my thumbs along his rough beard. "I mean, I've been without your lips for far too long."

It was like something in him roared to life then. He

reached for me eagerly, grasping my hips and lifting me into the air until I was straddling him. A peal of laughter escaped me. He used to always do this, toss me around on the grass as if I weighed nothing.

I'd loved it. I still did.

I looked down at him, my hair falling like a curtain around us as my lips hovered above his.

"I've ached for you since that day my brother forced me to leave," he confessed and my heart constricted. All these years I'd told myself he wasn't my mate, my future husband. He wasn't the one. Forget him. Hate him.

"Me too," I breathed and then our lips crashed together in a blind passion. This was no teenage love kiss. There was no tempered desire. This was five years of pent-up yearning. I opened my lips as our tongues stroked together eagerly and he stood quickly, holding onto my waist tightly as he walked with me.

I didn't need to ask where he was going. The bed. Tomorrow I could die fighting Ivanna and so tonight would be just for us, to make up for all the nights we'd slept alone. His fingers slipped up the back of my tunic as he explored my body and I gripped the back of his neck, pressing my lips harder into his.

There was nothing quite like your first love. Your heart fell faster and harder, without restraint, and every love after that paled in comparison. Axil was the man I'd compared every other guy to. The impossible figure for any man to model themselves after. And now I had the real thing.

His legs knocked against something and I pulled away from kissing him for a moment to find that we'd reached the bed. Without hesitation I pulled my top off and let my breasts spring free. His gaze hooded as he took me in fully.

Then he reached forward and kissed the smattering of freckles on my collarbone that he always traced with his finger, the spot that haunted me for years when I saw it in my reflection.

A small cluster of freckles that he particularly loved.

"I'm sorry for taking so long," he breathed. "But I promise to spend forever making it up to you." I fell back on the bed then, pulling off my trousers as he dropped his own. Everything about this was forbidden and I didn't care.

Our forever might just be tonight, for tomorrow I might go to meet the Maker. But even one night with Axil Moon was better than five years without him.

8

Laying with Axil and then sleeping next to him all night felt like something out of a dream. I'd imagined it so many times in my teenage years and even after. He was far more tender than I fantasized but also passionate. I tried to slip out of the bed quietly and leave, but he growled and it made me smile.

"Don't you dare bed me and then leave without breakfast," he scolded.

I laughed for falling into my usual ways with men. I had only bedded two others but it was casual and there was no breakfast involved.

"Well, you better hurry, I have a fight to win," I told him.

He crawled across the bed and yanked my hand, forcing me to fall on top of him laughing.

Reaching out, he traced my hairline, looking into my eyes with a tenderness I never remembered being there at fifteen. Perhaps that came in his two years of imprisonment. It was like he was grateful for the smallest things.

"You're damn straight you do."

That caused me to grin. "So ... you think I'll win?" I couldn't help the smile that pulled at my cheeks.

"I've seen you fight, Zara. Even when we were kids you were the strongest woman I'd ever met. You're a survivor. I have no doubt you are the toughest amongst the wolven and *will* be my queen."

I wanted to be happy about his compliment but instead bile rose in my throat. My mind was infiltrated of an image of sweet Eliza lying dead at my feet. I knew that my physical strength was unmatched against her ... but I had an emotional weakness where that girl was concerned. My packmate. My sister. I could never hurt a hair on her head.

"I need to get training," I said suddenly.

He must have noticed the shift in my mood and released me, nodding.

A servant came by with breakfast and we ate quickly and then I kissed him goodbye. I needed to get in the right headspace for this fight and being around Axil was not going to do that. I didn't want to spend too much time with my prize before I'd won it and lose my edge.

"WE'VE GOT THIS," I told Eliza and she nodded, though she looked like she might be sick.

The crowd had amassed again for our doubles fight. Two more girls had made it in from the outskirts just before the cut-off time: everyone else was assumed dead. Now whoever won this fight between Ivanna, Charlize and us, would fight the girls who'd just made it back. They were dehydrated and injured so it wasn't much of a competition.

Axil sat on his throne, high above the fighting ring, as I looked my brother in the eyes. I trusted him to get me through this and he always had sage advice, so I prepared myself to absorb whatever he was going to say now.

"You smell like him," my brother said and looked up at the king.

I stiffened at his words, blushing and then kicking myself for not bathing after bedding Axil.

That was not what I'd expected Cyrus to say.

Leaning into me, my brother whispered, "Use that. Get in Ivanna's head that you've already won the king."

Then he pulled back and I swallowed hard, giving him a curt nod. Mind games. His specialty. Instead of taunting her about sleeping with her coach, I was going to flaunt who I was bedding. What could go wrong?

Eliza's coach reached out and placed a hand on both Eliza's and my shoulders, bringing us closer together. "Use your pack link and the fact that Eliza is the biggest wolf here."

We both nodded: it had always been our strategy to use Eliza's large-sized wolf. Her size was a great asset.

I turned to Eliza. "Do you drink mead?"

She frowned, looking confused. "Not really. I'm more of a glass of wine girl ... when appropriate of course."

I grinned. She was adorable and so proper. "Tonight, after we win, we get so drunk we forget our names," I told her.

Her coach clicked his tongue in disapproval at my words.

That caused a smile to rise on Eliza's lips and I watched as her anxiety fled. "Deal."

We were ready.

I stepped into the ring, taking the sword that the advisor offered. I would not be stupid this time and decline a weapon. Not against Ivanna. He offered one to the opposing team and Ivanna picked it up. It looked like we had a similar strategy. We would stay human and protect our partner while they shifted to wolf form.

The bell hadn't rung yet, but I hefted the weight of the blade in my hands, not daring to look at Axil for fear of losing my concentration. I wouldn't allow my mind to waver, I had to be ruthless and unforgiving until these two women were either dead at my feet or on their knees crying forfeit.

The advisor raised his hand to quiet the crowd. "This fight must start human, only one partner can use the weapon and only one partner can shift into wolf form. This includes partial shifting." He looked at Ivanna and me.

We both nodded and Ivanna stepped closer to me, her nostrils flaring as she seemed to take in my scent. Her gaze flicked to Axil and then back to me and she growled.

I fake yawned. "I'm *so* tired. Last night was pretty wild." I chose that moment to look at Axil and wink and then the bell rang.

I barely had time to look back at Ivanna and she was advancing on me with a battle cry. I did something insane then, something to put myself at risk but make sure we won this. Cranking my arm back, I chucked the sword right at Ivanna's partner Charlize as she attempted to change into her wolf form. The blade left my fingers and sank into the girl's chest, knocking her backwards onto the ground.

She instantly bled out, sword sticking out of her chest. A death blow.

We were halfway there.

The assembled wolves went wild at my bold move.

There was no time to celebrate. I was unarmed now, Eliza was mid-shift behind me, and Ivanna was full of rage intent on driving that steel into my neck. I barely ducked out of the way as the blade whooshed over my head. I dove into Ivanna's abdomen, taking her to the ground and praying she would drop the sword in the process.

She didn't. We crashed onto the hard dirt and then she took the butt of the weapon and smashed it into my back repeatedly. Agony exploded across my back as I fought to pin her arms down but she was like a wild beast, thrashing down on me from all angles.

Hurry up, Eliza!

Rearing my head back, I slammed my forehead into Ivanna's and she cried out in pain as the crowd roared their approval. Suddenly Ivanna's hips thrust upward so hard that I was thrown off her and onto my side.

I hit the solid ground and then Ivanna tried to pull the sword up between us. Reaching out, I grabbed a handful of fine dirt and threw it right in her face. She coughed and sputtered and then I scrambled to get up to my feet.

Eliza ran to my side in her giant wolf form and I nearly sighed in relief.

Ivanna stood before us, holding her sword aloft and blinking her eyes rapidly to clear the dirt.

Eliza gave me a warning yip but I had already seen Ivanna making her move and turned in that direction.

She was headed right for me with the sword held out, and I knew I'd have to get a little injured so that Eliza could finish her. I'd worked through hundreds of battle scenarios over the years with my brother. We'd run drills since I was a young pup. I was made for this. But this scenario, being stuck in human form with someone coming at you with a blade when you were unarmed, was the worst.

Control where your opponent hurts you. My brother's advice came back to me as if floating on a memory cloud.

This was going to hurt but I had no choice. Reaching out with my hands, I grasped the blade with my fingers and squeezed as hard as possible to stop the weapon from goring my stomach. The crowd gasped, and even Axil's voice was among them. Red-hot pain flared to life between my fingers and I couldn't help the wail of agony that ripped from my throat. My wolf wanted freedom but I had to suppress her as per the fight rules. My natural instinct was to let go of the blade and end the misery, but I forced myself to hold onto it in an effort to keep my guts in my stomach.

I held Ivanna's murderous gaze as she screamed in my face, pushing the hilt of the blade with all her might. When Eliza's shadow passed over Ivanna, her face went slack and I looked away as Eliza took Ivanna's head into her giant jaws and ripped it from her body.

Her skull hit the ground with a thud and Ivanna's body stayed standing for a moment, which horrified me.

I dropped the blade, my bloody hands shaking as her legs finally crumpled and her body fell to the floor.

The way of our people was something that had gone

on for centuries, it was raw, animalistic and instinctual but that didn't mean I wasn't traumatized by it.

I looked at Eliza, the blood staining her mouth, and read the horror in her expression. We'd survived but we would never be the same after this.

All the mead in the realm wouldn't wipe that memory from our minds but I was sure as Hades going to try. The crowd was chanting our names, and then Cyrus was there with clean linens on my hands while Eliza shifted to human form. I flinched as he patched me up, pressing down flaps of skin over my palms that had been cut. Then I moved my gaze to Axil. There was pride in his eyes but it was mixed with something else.

Fear.

What was he scared of? Our next fight would be hard with me injured but I heard the girls were near dead so it wasn't going to be that difficult.

Axil cleared his throat to make an announcement and the wolves quieted.

"The third team that made it back from the dead lands and was supposed to fight the winners has fled to Cinder Mountain, forfeiting—"

Boos filled the space and a shock ran through me.

"They are now outcasts and will be torn apart if they ever return. That makes Eliza and Zara our final two champions."

I knew now why he looked fearful.

Nausea roiled through me as I came to the realization that my next fight would be against her. My pack sister.

No.

She seemed to realize it at the same moment.

"I won't," she said quietly beside me and my brother stiffened.

I nodded. "I won't either. Don't think of it. For now, we celebrate."

She dipped her chin, but the sickness in my stomach didn't leave me.

The mead started to flow then, the packs from all over began to pour it down my throat since I couldn't use my bandaged hands.

Every hour on the hour Eliza and I were hoisted into the air and carried around the tented field while everyone chanted, "Champions."

By the fourth pint of mead, Eliza and I were cackling in laughter at any small thing. Axil had even come to join the party which had assembled at the bonfire in front of my tent. It was hard to get drunk as a shifter: we burned it off too quickly, but I was well and truly buzzed right now.

"You throwing the dirt in her eyes was so cool!" a little wolven girl told me. "I'm using that move one day when I'm chosen as champion."

I smiled at her. "We'll make sure you have a good coach." I tried not to slur and the little girl nodded.

Her mother gave me a knowing smile and told the child it was time for bed.

By the time two more hours had passed, it was late and most everyone else had gone to sleep. Eliza, Cyrus, Axil and I were stomping around the fire in a circle, singing songs of old while shaking our half-drunk pints of mead. Everything felt numb and good and the blood-soaked gauze on my hands was a distant memory. A few wolven from my pack were playing songs on the drums when Axil asked me to dance.

Eliza knew that my heart belonged to him and so I knew she wouldn't mind if we danced. Though relationships with the king were forbidden, surely a dance wouldn't prove anything to anyone.

I threw my arms around his neck, careful of my healing hands as he gripped my waist and we swayed to the music. With the mead flowing through my system, I had no filter left to cover my words.

"I never stopped loving you," I whispered into his ear as he gripped me tightly. "Even when I hated you, I loved you."

There had been an Axil-sized hole in my heart that was never going to be healed by anyone except him.

His lips brushed against my ear. "I've loved you from that first day at camp, Zara," he said and my stomach fluttered. "And that's why you have to kill Eliza tomorrow."

My body went rigid and I pulled back with wide eyes. I shook my head vigorously and Axil leaned his forehead against mine. "Only the last wolf standing can be my wife, Zara," he said and the mead suddenly flushed from my system. Sobriety, mixed with horror, rushed through me.

Could I kill her? To be with the love of my life?

I glanced across the fire to see Eliza laughing and with my older brother. She was so carefree, her smile so genuine and her laugh full of such innocence. She wasn't made for this competition and yet somehow, she had fought her way to the top.

A sister for a husband?

I dropped my hands from around Axil's neck and took a step back. "I'm beat. I need some sleep," I told him.

Concern flashed across his face and he nodded. "Do you want to come to my—"

I shook my head. "I'll sleep with my pack. Last night," I said.

Tomorrow I would be dead, or his wife.

He nodded, swallowing hard, and Eliza's laughter died down as she looked over at me. "Going to bed?"

I bobbed my head. "I'm exhausted," I lied. I probably wouldn't sleep a wink. Killing someone I had grown so close to wasn't something I was sure I was capable of.

She frowned.

The tension of our reality hung in the air like a tangible thing. Axil took two steps towards Eliza. "Come see me first thing in the morning, Eliza. I'll break your temporary pack bond and take you back into Death Mountain pack."

Temporary? That hurt and yet I knew it had to be

done. I couldn't fight a packmate to the death. It was insane.

Her face was completely void of any emotion and she just nodded.

The drums had stopped and my brother seemed to pick up on the awkwardness of this whole thing. "Well, we should get to bed. Goodnight, everyone," he said to all those who still lingered at the bonfire and then walked over to me, physically pushing me inside our tent.

I looked up at my big brother with tears swimming in my eyes and was surprised to see that he too looked emotional.

"Cyrus, I can't," I whimpered.

He released a shaky breath. "You have to, Zara."

I didn't sign up for this, to kill someone I cared about!

I tore across the tent and then slipped into my hammock, covering my face with the fur blanket so that I could hide from the world.

It wasn't fair and I couldn't do it. I heard the hissing of the fire as my brother put it out with a bucket of water and then my packmates whispered as they bid each other goodnight. They all slipped into their hammocks as I lay awake, the buzz of the mead fully worn off thanks to my rapid healing. My hands barely hurt anymore, already mending, and my mind was a complete mess. I was plagued with memories of Axil and our love story. Who meets their mate at fifteen years old? But then my mind would bring up memories of Eliza. How she'd done nothing but protect me and watch my back since I got here. She needed me.

Like Axil had said, I was nothing if not loyal. But who should I be loyal to? My love for Axil? Or for Eliza? I tossed and turned for hours, long after Cyrus and the others fell into a deep slumber and started snoring.

I just lay there, my mind spiraling as I stared out of the open flap of the tent and looked up at the moon.

Maker, help me. I prayed for the first time in a long time. This was too much to bear.

9

I knew I wouldn't sleep; I'd come to terms with that. Instead, I just lay awake as the hours ticked by. Footsteps sounded outside and I perked up when I saw a shadow cross over the tent. Suddenly Eliza was standing in the doorway and for a wild second I thought she meant to assassinate me before our fight and I welcomed it.

Take the decision from me and just end it all, I begged.

But she wasn't holding a weapon and she looked like she'd been crying. She walked right up to my hammock, staring down at me.

"Can't sleep?" she whispered to me.

I shook my head and she nodded that I should follow her outside. I sat up, stepping out of the hammock and followed her into the crisp cool night. It was chilly and so I pulled my fur cloak on to keep me warm.

"What's up?" I asked, praying she wouldn't beg me to spare her life.

She turned to face me with an eerie calmness. "I said goodbye to my family a few hours ago and then tried to escape to Cinder Mountain," she said flatly and I gasped.

"You wha— what happened?" I looked at her more closely now, noticing some dirt and cuts on her arms.

She sighed. "The advisors have the entire mountain surrounded by Royal Guards. After the other two girls fled, no one can get out. They want their last fight, they want their queen."

My heart broke then. She'd tried to leave, to give me a chance to win without anyone getting killed. She failed.

"Eliza, I can't—"

She held up a hand and then finally met my gaze. "I never expected to make it this far," she said with a smile. "My family understands the situation and tomorrow I'm going to forfeit."

My eyes flew wide. "You can't, you'll be ripped apart!"

She looked inside the pack tent and then pulled me farther away so that I wouldn't wake anyone.

"*I'll* forfeit," I told her boldly.

She shook her head. "Then *you* get ripped apart and *I*

marry Axil. Do you really want me bedding him for the rest of my life?"

A growl formed in my throat and she chuckled. "That's what I thought. You guys are mates. You're the stronger of the two of us. You *deserve* to be queen."

An unexpected sob shook my body and she pulled me in for a bone-crushing hug. I cried then, for what felt like the tenth time since I got to this damn mountain and she held me, keeping her composure the entire time.

"You're so calm," I told her as I pulled away.

She nodded. "I've made my peace with the situation, Zara. Come on, I want to show you my favorite place in the whole city. When you are queen, you can go there to watch the sunrise and remember me."

Hooking her elbow into mine, she pulled me after her, but my mind was still playing catch-up.

Remember her.

She wanted me to remember her because she was going to die? I walked in a numb silence beside her as we hiked around the castle and up the mountain that loomed behind it. She'd already made peace with her own pack tearing her apart? And I was supposed to sit by and watch it happen?

"Eliza—"

"Shh, I want my last night to be happy," she cut me off and another sob lodged in my throat. We hiked, arm in arm past a few Royal Guards for a good twenty minutes until we reached a flat bench of rock. There we sat and looked out onto the moonlight which lit up the vast expanse of land.

It was dark, with only the moonlight to illuminate it and yet it was still so pretty. From this vantage point I could see the dozens of patrolling guards all around the perimeter of the mountain. We were stuck here. Our fate was sealed.

"I'm glad it's you," Eliza said finally, startling me. We'd been sitting next to each other in silence for some time.

I looked at her and she was peering at the castle below and the city that stretched out beyond.

"I'm glad you will be our people's queen."

I didn't know what to say to that. I still wasn't sure I was okay with what she was doing. Forfeiting to me and getting torn apart? There had to be another way.

"Maybe if those two girls who ran off were found—"

Eliza reached out and grasped my fingers to quiet me, then she leaned back on the rock and I followed her, lying on my back and looking up at the stars.

"When I was younger it was hard for me to make friends. You know how it is being a dominant female," she said.

I nodded because I did know. The other dominant girls saw you as competition and the submissives were too scared to be around you for too long. You ended up hanging with the guys most of the time yet still feeling lonely.

"I never really felt like I belonged here. But when you

took me into Mud Flat pack ... it was hard to describe." I looked over at her. She was smiling wistfully up at the stars. "I felt, for the first time like I had a *real* pack family and a sisterhood." She squeezed my hand.

I hated this. I hated that she was saying goodbye.

"I'll figure something out," I told her but I knew my words were a lie. What was there to do? Stop a tradition that was over a thousand years old? We'd both be torn apart. The wolven people needed a strong queen and this was how they chose her. I was as much a victim to the circumstance as Eliza was.

We continued to hold hands as the night dragged on and sleep pulled at my limbs. It must only have been a few hours before sunrise but I could feel the heaviness of exhaustion pressing down on me. Eliza's breathing evened out and I closed my eyes, only for a second, and fell asleep.

"Wake up. Look!" Eliza's voice infiltrated my brain and my eyelids snapped open. I was disoriented for a moment, wondering where I was and why I was being woken. I could easily go for another ten hours' sleep. Thick grogginess weighed me down but then I remembered I'd fallen asleep on the rock with Eliza and today was our fight.

I sprang into a sitting position and gasped when I saw what was before me. The realm that was once bathed in darkness was now covered with oranges and pinks across the entire horizon. The sunlight kissed the land as far as the eye could see and I was shocked at how far the visibility stretched from here. I could almost see the edge of the Mud Flats, blurry in the distance.

I looked over at Eliza to see a single tear slide down her cheek. She was so filled with life and innocence, I just couldn't allow that to be extinguished. It was in this moment that I realized she would make an amazing queen. The love of her people and this land was exactly what a queen should have. I reached out and squeezed her hand, coming to terms with my own future just as she did.

"Isn't it beautiful?"

I nodded. "Breathtaking."

We sat in silence for another few moments and then the people began to move down below, stoking their fires and cooking their breakfast.

"Axil wanted to see me," she said.

I nodded. "I'll go with you."

We stood and then made our way off the mountain and past the guards who watched us carefully, a hand on the blade at their hip.

When we reached the front doors of the castle, the guard stepped aside without question and let us in. We were instructed to go to the dining hall where we found Axil sitting in front of an untouched plate of food.

It seemed we weren't the only ones preoccupied about the battle to come. Eliza was *his* wolf; he'd grown up with her. Knowing I had to kill her to be with him couldn't have sat well with him.

"Eliza, Zara, thanks for coming." He plastered on a fake smile as we approached.

Eliza stood before him and extended her wrist. "I think this will be easier on all of us if I rejoin Death Mountain pack before the fight."

Axil's fake smile faltered but he nodded. "I agree."

Then he looked at me, as if asking if it were okay. It was hard to explain but I felt like Eliza's alpha. I didn't really know how all that worked since Dorian was my alpha but ... she felt like *mine*.

I bit the inside of my cheek and nodded. For some reason I was sad. I didn't want to feel the gaping hole left behind by her, the same hole that any pack member left when they went to marry and join another pack. But she ... she was mine, I'd claimed her and we'd worked together to stay alive out there in the dead lands.

Axil shifted his fingers to claws and dragged them across her arm, forcing blood to come to the surface. Then he scratched his own arm, mixing the blood.

My heart beat wildly in my chest and I could feel Eliza's hesitation. She didn't want to do this either. She was Mud Flat pack now and it felt so right. But I'd taken her in as a pack sister without permission of my alpha, or hers, and so I knew this must be done.

Axil mumbled under his breath and I felt a sharp sudden squeezing at my heart, Eliza gasped and I knew she'd felt it too. I looked at Axil and his brows were drawn into a knot at the center of his forehead. He mumbled words under his breath and again I felt that pain in my heart but Eliza was still there. I felt her strength and innocence.

Axil released a shaky breath and then stared at me. "Your bond is too strong. I can't take her back."

Eliza had this resigned look on her face but I felt horrified by the whole thing. It was just proof that we were family now.

"Will you give us a moment?" I asked her.

She nodded, squeezing my shoulder as she passed. "I'll go see my parents and sister one last time and then meet you in the ring."

Bile rose in my throat at that and then she left. The second the door closed, I rushed into Axil's space. "I can't, Axil. I won't. I love you but I can't kill her."

He swallowed hard, nodding. "She's going to forfeit."

I froze. "How did you know?"

"She came to me late last night and told me." He looked sick as well. "And I haven't slept since. I never expected her to make it this far to be honest. You made her stronger, you turned her into a tough contender."

I did. I prolonged the inevitable. Stupid me.

"Can you ... I don't know, talk to the advisors? Axil, she's my packmate, the trials are supposed to be one woman from each pack."

He wouldn't meet my gaze, he was staring at his plate of food. "I tried. An hour ago. They said the strongest woman must be queen and that's why the trials were designed this way. The people will accept nothing less."

I reached up and rubbed the back of my neck. "What if you call off the trial? Don't get married." I suddenly blurted out. "I don't need to be queen, I can just be your lover, in secret—"

He pulled me into his arms then and my throat tightened. "They will not let me remain king without a queen and eventually an heir."

Right. The bloodline must go on.

I let him hold me, releasing all the tension I was carrying since Eliza and I had killed Ivanna and Charlize. Either way, no matter how you sliced it, Eliza or I were going to die today.

"Can you make it a law that you can forfeit but still keep your life?"

Axil looked at me as if I were a small child. "That *is* the law. It's the people who have taken it upon themselves to kill a pack member for forfeiting."

I felt trapped.

Pulling back from him, I finally forced him to meet my gaze. "Tell me what to do," I begged.

Let her forfeit? Should I forfeit? Try to run and let the guards kill me? I just needed someone else to make the decision for me, to take away the burden.

He frowned. "You really love her, don't you? Like a sister?"

I nodded. "I never should have befriended her. But it's

too late now. And she saved my life out there in the dead lands. She's so loyal and innocent—"

He reached up and traced my bottom lip, stopping my words. "I'm selfish. I want you as my wife and queen, so do not ask me what you should do. I will disappoint you."

I frowned at that but appreciated the honesty.

Reaching out, he traced my jawline with his finger. "Do what you can live with and I will make sure we are together."

I chewed my lip. How could he make sure we were together if I forfeited and then got ripped apart by my pack? He was daydreaming about a scenario that didn't exist.

I knew I had to get out of there and yet I wasn't ready to say goodbye to Axil. I wished we'd had more time, more kisses, more everything.

Because as much as I loved Axil and wanted to be with him, there was no way in Hades I was letting Eliza die on my account. I would forfeit, the crowd would tear me apart and Eliza would be queen. Would Axil love her like he loved me? No. Not at first, but I hoped they could grow to love each other in their own way and offer companionship.

There were no words for this situation so I let my body do the talking. Reaching up, I grasped Axil's chin and pulled his mouth to mine. His body immediately responded and his fingers clutched my hips, pressing me tightly to him. My mouth opened as his tongue slid across mine and my heart actually ached in this moment. Kissing Axil was like breathing and I didn't know how I had gone so long without it, without him. My inner fifteen-year-old lovesick little teenager had secretly prayed for this moment. For our reunification, and now ... it was over.

A single tear slipped down my cheek and landed on our locked lips, tracing our kiss and sealing it forever.

He stiffened then.

He knew.

He knew what my choice would be.

Pulling back, I kissed his nose and gave him a weak smile. "I love you, Axil Moon. Now. Forever. Always," I said and then I stepped back, his hands falling away from me as his face went slack. I couldn't look at him anymore and so I turned and left the room, walking away from him like he walked away from me when I was fifteen.

I wanted to cry, but that was a weakness I couldn't afford right now. I needed to go out into this crowd and look as strong as possible. And so I sucked all of my storming emotions down and traversed the hallways, making my way outside. The second I approached my pack's tent, I felt my knees go weak.

"Zara!" Oslo ran for me and then crashed into my stomach, wrapping his arms around my middle.

No. Not him. My gaze searched the crowd of people now in front of my tent to see that Dorian, Amara and nearly the entire pack had come.

No.

Oslo pulled back and looked up at me. "Are you surprised to see us?" he asked, giving me a huge smile.

I was in shock, my heart fluttering as I imagined my little brother watching Dorian rip out my throat.

I couldn't speak.

Dorian saw me then and grinned. "When I heard you'd made it to the final fight, I had to be here." He stepped over and lifted me into the air. Normally I would smile, or say something snarky but again, I was speechless.

Dorian sensed it then, something restless in my soul. He set me down, frowning, and met my gaze.

"All well, little wolf?"

I swallowed hard, glancing around at my packmates nervously.

"Let's give them some space," Amara said and the pack cleared the firepit area, clapping me on the back as they passed.

When it was just Cyrus and Dorian, I looked my alpha in the eyes and held his stare.

"You heard I brought one of the girls into Mud Flat pack to survive?" I asked him.

He nodded. "I felt it. Still do." He tapped his chest.

I figured. "Axil tried to break the bond this morning and take her back. He couldn't. It's too strong."

My brother let a curse word fly and rubbed the back of his neck in anxiety but Dorian just nodded. "I see."

Did he? Did he know what I was about to do?

He opened his mouth to speak when I heard my name called and turned. One of the elder wolven advisors was standing behind me with two guards.

It was time and Dorian would find out my plan soon enough. Best not to worry him.

I turned back around and pulled the big alpha in for a hug. "You're a good man, Dorian, and you were a *great* alpha," I whispered into his ear as his arms tightened around me.

When I pulled back, he looked surprised at my words, his eyebrows knotted in the center of his forehead in confusion.

I walked over to my coach, my big brother, and pulled him in for a hug next. "Don't let Oslo see. Keep him in the tent," I told him and he nodded against my shoulder. Cyrus was clueless to my plan as well but he knew I was protective over my little brother and probably just thought I didn't want him to see me get injured or kill Eliza.

After turning from my pack, I followed the guards to the fighting ring. I had barely slept, I hadn't eaten and nausea rolled through my stomach as the crowd chanted my name. I looked up to see Axil sitting on his throne: today he wore the sharp-bladed crown of the king wolven. His brother Ansel stood beside him, glaring at me with his wife Jade at his side.

This would please his brother, to see that we would not end up together. His little brother and king would not marry Mud Flat trash after all.

I turned my attention to the center of the dirt circle to see Eliza, standing tall and beaming at me.

"No rules for this fight! Anything goes!" the elder advisor shouted behind me.

I walked right up to Eliza and placed my hands on her shoulders. "Be good to him," I told her and she frowned in confusion at my words.

The bell rang and I spun, giving Eliza my back.

I tipped my chin high and raised my voice for all to hear. "I have no doubt I am the strongest wolf in this ring. But Eliza Green is my packmate! We forged a bond so strong even the king himself could not tear it away."

There were shocked gasps from the onlookers and even howls as people stepped closer to me, knowing what I was about to do.

"And even though I've loved that man since I was fifteen," I pointed to Axil, "I cannot hurt my pack sister." Eliza crashed into me, wrapping her arms around me from behind, sobbing.

"No," she said but I ignored her.

"I, Zara Swiftwater of Mud Flat pack, for—"

"I step down as king!" Axil cried out, cutting off my words and my entire body went limp. I could barely hold myself up as shock ripped through me. The crowd shared my sentiment as they wavered on their feet, gasping, booing and screaming.

Dorian was so bowled over by the king's comment that

he spun his attention away from me and we both faced Axil.

"The law states that the Queen Trial must end if a king ever steps down from duty and hands his crown over," Axil said and then walked down from the throne and strode over to his brother and his brother's wife. Ansel was as still as a snake before it was about to strike. Axil faced him and took in a deep breath. "I'll give you back the title of Alpha King if you let Zara and I run away together. You will never see me again," he told him.

I knew then that he'd planned this all along, that if it looked like I might lose he'd always been ready to do this. His voice didn't shake, he was so calm, like he'd planned it for months.

The crowd's boos got louder and I didn't know if it was because they never liked Ansel and didn't want him as king again, or if they hated Axil's weak act of stepping down. As wolves we fought for dominance, we didn't give it away. But as a king within the royal bloodline and no heir, at least two of them needed to stay alive until Ansel had a child.

"I give you my word," Ansel said, looking to the royal wolven advisors who nodded one by one and relief washed over me.

The two brothers shook on it and then Axil took the sharp-bladed crown from his head and sliced his arm with it.

Ansel did the same and they shared blood on the

blade. I knew in that moment that the power to control every other wolven had just passed to Ansel. He was now king.

Ansel grinned as he took the crown and placed it on his head. Axil nodded to him, walking away from his brother as if he hadn't just given away an entire kingdom and birthright!

I peered at Dorian, wild-eyed, wondering if he would let me walk away from this. He must have known what I was about to do: to forfeit as a coward. And to run away with Axil meant I'd be leaving his pack. I'd need permission for that.

There was a softness in Dorian's gaze, one he usually lacked. With one curt nod from him, I rushed forward into Axil's arms and he lifted me off the ground, spinning me around.

The boos got louder and the crowd pushed in closer. They wanted their fight, not a forfeit and loss of their strongest king.

Ansel was a decent enough king but he now walked with a limp, which was seen as a weakness, and he was kind of cruel in my opinion.

"We need to get out of here," Axil whispered to me. "We can go to Thorngate. Lucien will hide us."

Lucien Thorne? The fae king?

I just nodded, trying to process it all as we pushed our way out of the crowd with Eliza, Cyrus, Dorian and my other packmates keeping the mass at bay.

"We don't want Ansel as our king!" someone yelled.

"You coward!" another spat.

"King coward!"

"Queen coward!"

Queen coward, I'd earned a nickname before even becoming queen. That might be a record.

But the crowd seemed split because as many people who'd tried to rush us and attack, that many or more pushed them out of the way.

"Let them go!"

"They have honor!"

"She was loyal to her pack sister!"

"They're mates!"

I absorbed everything going on as we made our way to the edge of the forest and the uncertainty that lay beyond. Flee to Thorngate? Leave our kind and the lands of Fallenmoore forever? It felt so wrong and yet when Axil slipped his fingers into mine, it felt so right.

I'd not really forfeited. Eliza wouldn't be harmed. Axil was no longer king but we would be together. Then why did something feel off: like I was leaving something important behind?

Just as I thought of him, Oslo screamed my name.

I spun, pulling free from Axil as my little brother crashed into me and I wrapped my arms around him.

"Take me with you. Please, I beg you," he pleaded, tears in his eyes.

I looked up at Axil, unsure what he would think of all

this. He knew my brother was almost like a son to me, and that I'd raised him after my parents died.

Axil simply nodded once and relief rushed through me. I glanced at Cyrus and Dorian who flanked us, keeping the crowd back and they both dipped their heads in agreement as well.

"Okay, you can come," I told Oslo and he pulled back from me with a grin, wiping at his leaking eyes.

I loved that boy too much. Axil would have to toughen him up for me because my heart was too soft when it came to him. He reminded me so much of our sweet mother.

Eliza pulled me in for a final hug. "Goodbye, sister," she whispered, her throat clogged with emotion and then I felt her, through our bond and all of the love and respect she had for me.

"What are you going to do?"

She shrugged. "Go live in the Mud Flats and marry one of your cute single packmates?"

I laughed at that and everything felt a little bit brighter. I'd have to find a way to get word to her. I never thought this would be a possibility, that Axil would step down as king and run away with me.

I could sense Axil's urgency; the crowd was getting restless and we needed to leave before there was an altercation.

With that, Axil grasped my hand once more and I held Oslo's with my other hand and we walked into the woods and our unknown future together.

We were about ten steps into the dense forest when my muscles suddenly constricted and it felt like I'd slammed into a wall. I stopped abruptly, gasping as an unknown power seized control over my limbs. I knew by the shocked inhale of breath beside me that the same thing had just happened to Axil.

"No," he breathed, slowly craning his neck to peer over at me wide-eyed.

My little brother looked up at us in confusion and I swallowed hard. "Run," I told Oslo and dropped his hand.

"Did you really think I would let you go?" Ansel's voice boomed behind us both and then without any effort of my own, I turned around to face him.

As a dominant wolf, being controlled by another person was literally my worst nightmare. I growled, fisting my knuckles and snarling, but it was no use. He had complete power over me.

The broken-up crowd suddenly loomed behind Ansel, my brother Cyrus included and my gaze frantically searched for Eliza and Dorian.

Why weren't they there? Did they try to fight the king and ...

Relief rushed through me when I saw them waving Oslo over to them as they snuck worried glances at their new king. Oslo wisely bolted from my side and King Ansel let him go. A small mercy.

"I gave you what you wanted," Axil growled beside me. "Let us go."

Ansel's eyes sharpened. "You think I wanted you to hand me my crown?" he seethed.

My heart raced in my chest and I pulled against the invisible force holding me captive to no avail.

"You should have killed me when you had the chance, brother," Ansel whispered, and I growled.

Ansel's head snapped in my direction and he grinned, sending a chill down my spine. The thing that scared me the most was that his eyes lacked humanity.

"You gave me your word!" Axil roared as pelts of fur rippled down his skin but he was forced to remain upright.

Ansel tipped his head back and laughed, a hollow and empty sound. "You were a fool to believe me."

The new wolf king then turned to a line of Royal Guards and tipped his head to them. "Bring my brother and his *lover* to the dungeon."

Axil and I shared a look. Axil appeared void of all emotion then, likely retreating into the dark memories in his mind of his two years in imprisonment.

This was bad, so bad. Could Ansel do this? He'd given his word in front of the wolven advisors. Yet they just stood behind him with their heads down. Was he controlling them too? If so, it was forbidden. The advisors kept the king from making bad choices: they were never to be controlled.

Eliza, Cyrus and Dorian all glared at Ansel as he passed and then my feet were thrust forward. I was like a puppet, putting one foot in front of the other as I followed the king. Eliza growled low in her throat as Ansel passed and he stopped to look at her. "Kneel," he taunted and Eliza bowed her head and fell to her knees forcefully.

He was abusing his power. This wasn't what the king's magic was to be used for. It was to break up fights, and command troops in time of war so that we could fight as if we were one being. Not this.

I wanted to scream, I wanted to tell Ansel what a monster he was but I knew Axil's life was in his hands, as well as my own, so I kept my mouth shut.

This was not how I expected this day to end.

We'd been strung up like fresh kills, hanging from our hands in shackles with my feet barely touching the ground. A collar was cinched around my throat which then had a metal leash attached and bolted to the stone ceiling to keep us from shifting forms. My arms ached, my wrists burned and I'd never been more livid in my entire life. We'd been put up on display right in the large private dining room of the castle. We'd never even been taken to the dungeon.

Ansel was sitting at the head of the table with his wife, eating a decadent meal while Axil and I starved.

He was taking psychological warfare to the extreme. His wife was from Ivanna's pack, a ruthless dominant who'd won her Queen Trials famously by choking the other girl with her bare hands. But they'd been married four years now, and no child? It meant the rumors of her being barren might be true.

"Let her go," Axil growled to his brother. "Let Zara go, she has nothing to do with this."

Ansel put down his fork and stood, walking over to where Axil hung on the far wall next to me. "Oh, she has everything to do with this, brother." He looked back at his wife. "Something's wrong with Jade. She can't give me children. So, I'll divorce her and take Zara as my wife. The moment she's pregnant with my heir, I'll kill you."

My gut clenched at his words and fear seized me. His wife hung her head in shame and that's when Axil went absolutely berserk.

He bucked against his chains and screamed and growled. The bolt in the ceiling that held the chains creaked and strained and fur popped out onto Axil's arms. It broke my heart to see him so helpless.

Ansel tipped his head back and laughed, walking back to the table as Axil went insane trying to free himself.

"Axil," I whispered and he stilled, panting. He looked over at me with eyes that were blue threaded through with yellow. I was speaking to man and beast. "Whatever happens, I will be okay," I told him and tried to keep the emotions off my face. I knew he would feel responsible for this. Giving Ansel control of the pack again and all the power that comes with being a king might seem stupid now, but we couldn't have known his brother would do this. He gave his word in front of every wolven present, including the advisors. A king was nothing if not a man of his word. Ansel was a coward in every way. Not strong enough to defeat Axil in a challenge fight, so he used the king's power to control him and get what he wanted.

Axil's jaw clenched, the veins in his neck bulging. "You will *not* be touched by him. I. Will. Kill. Him if he marries or beds you."

He didn't whisper. And Ansel heard. And he erupted into another laugh.

He's insane. That was clear to me now. And his wife, our queen, was acting like the most submissive dominant female I'd ever met. She just sat there and said nothing, like a stuffed toy.

He's controlling her too. The horror of that realization hit me like a punch to the stomach.

No.

He could cause a person to lose their self-control and he was doing that to her now. This was an insane abuse of power, yet, I was unable to stop it.

The dinner dragged on and I'd long lost feeling in my hands, my shoulders were numb as well. Any time my legs gave out, the collar choked me and forced me to stand right back up. I prayed we wouldn't be made to sleep like this. Was this what Ansel did to Axil when he was younger? No. A person couldn't live like this for two years. This was for show. This was for Ansel to prove he had all the power.

Just as King Ansel was wiping his mouth and had eaten his last bite, the doors to the dining hall opened.

I looked up, bleary-eyed and in pain.

A guard stepped in and cleared his throat. "My lord, you have three visitors outside who claim to be the queens of Thorngate, Archmere and Embergate."

My heart beat wildly in my chest and I exchanged a shocked glance with Axil.

Ansel picked up his mead and took a long swig, letting the silence stretch in the room. "Send them in," he stated at last.

Why would the queens of other realms come here, to Fallenmoore? If they had a message, they would send it with a courier. To come in person meant something was gravely wrong. Maybe something to do with that war meeting Axil had had. I'd never even asked about it, I'd been so consumed with winning the trials.

A moment later, three beautiful women entered the room, one of them carrying a small tin box in her hands. They were bright-eyed and smiling until their gazes landed on us. All three of their smiles were wiped from their faces at the sight. In that moment the brown-haired human-looking one slipped the tin box into her cloak and bowed deeply to Ansel.

"King Axil Moon?" she asked Ansel. "We are so pleased to meet y—"

"I'm King *Ansel*. My brother Axil is no longer king." He jerked his head in our direction.

The women remained tight lipped, with forced smiles, betraying only slight signs of anxiety.

The red-headed fae stepped forward, not bowing, and held the king's gaze. "I am the Fae Queen Madelynn of Thorngate: we have come bearing grave news and seek your help, King Ansel."

Grave news.

Axil stiffened beside me as we watched the scene unfold. I noticed the blonde one, I was guessing dragon-folk, stood there poised as if ready to attack and did not take her gaze off Ansel.

"What *grave* news?" Ansel asked as he stood back from the table. His wife still had her head bowed and it killed me to think he was doing that to her. How powerful was he? Could he control all of us if we were to attack him at once?

The redhead, Queen Madelynn, cleared her throat. "The Nightfall queen has been stealing your wolves and using a magical device to siphon their power and give it to her people to drink as an elixir. She then uses this power to attack us at our borders."

Holy Hades! *What?*

Ansel looked unfazed. "How unfortunate for you."

The blonde queen's eyes narrowed and the brunette tightened her fists.

A slight breeze picked up in the room, which I found odd, and Queen Madelynn took one step closer to the king. "If we cannot defeat the Nightfall queen, she will ride north, to Fallenmoore, and take you all out," she declared. "We plead for assistance in this war."

King Ansel grinned and chills raced across my skin. "Let her try. I will bring her to her knees and make her cut her own throat. Just as I can do with you."

I barely had time to register the shock of his threat when a window broke on the far wall and a roaring wind blew into the room creating a funnel. The blonde dragon-folk queen raised her hands as if to attack King Ansel but just as soon as the wind had come and these three women had attempted their attack, they all grabbed their heads in unison, screaming as they bowed on their knees.

He's controlling them too. This shook me to my core. I looked at Axil, unbelieving that he had had this kind of power the entire time.

No one should be this formidable. It was terrifying.

Ansel looked back at his brother with a grin. "Should I kill them?"

No! I wanted to scream but suddenly my throat felt paralyzed. He was keeping me from speaking.

"If you do, the kings of Avalier will come for you and you'll have a war on your hands with multiple foes," Axil said calmly.

Ansel nodded. "Maybe they can stay the night and I'll decide if I should kill them or send them on their way tomorrow." He tapped his chin as if thinking.

He looked at his guards posted around the room. "Ready the dungeon."

Those three words were terrifying and yet if I was about to be released from this torture device, I didn't care where I went.

The three queens hissed and groaned, on their knees as Ansel continued whatever torment he was doing to them and my heart broke for the women. They'd come all this way to plead for help and now this. It was awful and Ansel was playing with fire by attacking them, though I was pretty sure the fae queen had attacked first with that wind. I'd heard about the fae being able to control certain elements, and I'd just seen it firsthand. She'd broken that window somehow and pulled the wind inside. It made me wonder what the other women could do. I was sheltered in the sense that I'd never left Fallenmoore but I'd heard many stories about the powers of the other races.

"Let's take a walk and put all of our guests up for the night, shall we, darling?" Ansel called to his wife who stood, head bowed as she turned stiffly, without much animation.

Two of the guards left, but the other two walked over to Axil and me. When one of them reached up to unhook the chain from the ceiling bolt, I cried out in pain at the sudden movement as relief then spread throughout my limbs. Then my neck collar chain was released too and I whimpered at being free of the hanging position. My arms fell limply to my sides and then all of my weight was suddenly on my feet. My legs could no longer hold me up after hours of fatigue and I felt myself falling. But I never did. As if driven by an unseen force, I pulled my leg out from under me to stabilize myself and then I was walking. The chain from the collar at my neck dragged behind me as I followed King Ansel, his wife, and the three queens. We all marched in a perfect line, with flawlessly spaced steps. All against our will.

I wanted to look behind me and see if Axil was following but I couldn't move my head. Ansel was controlling every muscle in my body and it terrified me. Had I known he was capable of *this*, I never would have allowed Axil to step down and give Ansel such power. I didn't think Axil would have done it either. It seemed that his brother had snapped and had never before used his power over people to this degree.

We walked down the hall and to a wide stone staircase that led to a damp dungeon with gray stone walls and no light. Every once in a while the wind would brush past me lightly only to die out and Ansel would laugh. I assumed the fae queen was trying to use her power. He'd taken my voice: I was completely helpless and it made me feel sick.

When we turned the corner, I saw one wrought-iron door standing open. My heart picked up speed as one by one we marched into the cell against every effort to stay out. When Ansel used his power to turn me around, I watched in relief as Axil walked in after me.

Ansel's wife stood still at his side, head down, hair limply covering her face. I found myself wondering why she hadn't killed him over the last two years, when he was without this power and Axil was king? Maybe he'd never done this to her before and it was new behavior. I surely could never let a man live after this kind of treatment.

We all stood in a large cell, spread out in a line as Ansel walked slowly inside and right up to Queen Madelynn. He grinned as he looked her up and down, and again a light gust of wind blew past us and then died out.

"I find your rebellion *extremely* attractive," he told her, and I forced a growl into my throat, working past his power. How dare he flirt with a married queen! This level of disrespect looked bad on all wolven. He was shaming our entire culture with this treatment of these monarchs.

Ansel's head snapped in my direction and my stomach dropped. He walked calmly over to me and then leaned in, letting his nose rest against my neck. Pulling in a deep lungful of air, he inhaled. "My brother's whore," he whispered, and Axil growled next to me but the noise was cut off with a whimper as he fell to the floor, grasping at his head and screaming in pain.

Tears leaked out of the corners of my eyes as the realization that we were all puppets to a sick man hit me.

"Come on, let's go make an heir," Ansel said to me and fear seized me in its grip.

The wind picked up again, stronger this time and Axil went mad with his screaming. The blonde queen next to me started blowing a stream of smoke out of her nostrils and all Ansel did was laugh as he stepped out of the cell and made me follow him.

12

Axil

The pain in my head, which felt like someone had taken an axe to my skull, was nothing compared to the agony in my heart. Ansel had just left the dungeon cell with the love of my life.

To bed her.

The farther their footsteps retreated, the less of a hold my brother had on me and the others.

The others.

I was locked in a cell with my childhood best friends' wives. It was surreal. When I finally felt the pain in my head dissipate and the use of my legs and muscles return, I turned to the three woman who were now moving their arms and fingers in front of them.

"What the Fae was that?" Madelynn, the redhead said. I appraised my best friend Lucien's new wife. She had some type of wind magic and she was powerful enough to use it minimally even under Ansel's command. It was impressive.

"That was awful!" the brunette, who smelled like a human-elf mixture, stated. "I want to skin him alive."

The blonde was eerily still, she merely cocked her head and looked at me. "Was that your mate?" There was smoke streaming out of her nostrils and my heart pinched at the word *mate*.

A low growl emanated from my throat and I fisted my hands, forcing my wolf to stay down so I could speak to these women. "Yes. And I need to get to her before he ..." My words died in my throat and I spun, wrapping my hands around the bars at the door and shaking them. It was no use, I knew that. I'd lived in this cell for two years. This was where Ansel broke people down, though he'd never displayed the blatant disregard for others' freewill like he did tonight. He must have finally snapped.

"Yeah, that's not happening. We're getting out of here," Madelynn said bluntly, and the wind picked up, swirling around me. I turned to her and was surprised to find her just as angry as I was.

The blonde, who I was assuming from the smoking nostrils was the dragon queen, walked over to me. "I'm Arwen, queen of the dragon-folk and we're going to help you get your mate back, okay?"

I could only nod, in shock at what was happening.

"And I'm Kailani," the brown-haired woman said. "Elf queen."

Arwen then walked over to the fae queen Madelynn and looked her dead in the eyes. "Can you take care of the guard?"

Madelynn nodded and then stepped over to me. "Move, please. We don't have much time."

I stumbled away from the door dumbfounded as she held up her hand in front of the bars.

"Are you hurt?" The elf queen was there beside me, inspecting my bleeding wrists.

"I'll heal. It's fine," I told her, wondering when Raife had married her. He didn't seem the marrying type the last time we spoke, which admittedly was years ago. I was slightly hurt there was no wedding invite to any of these marriages but I couldn't really blame them. We'd all fallen out of touch when Raife's family was murdered by the Nightfall queen.

I was watching the fae queen with a keen interest. She didn't appear to be doing anything and yet I heard the sounds of struggling just outside the cell. Someone was gasping for—

"You're stealing the air from his lungs?" I asked in shock as the realization hit me.

She looked over at me with a raised eyebrow and nodded. "The same thing I will do to your brother now that I know what he's capable of," she snarled.

Wow, she must be a fall fae to have wind magic. I had no idea the kind of power a wind fae could have, until now. I'd never really thought about it. Lucien could freeze people to death and she could steal the air from their lungs: they were quite the pair. As long as these women helped me get Zara back without harm, I didn't care what they did to anyone else.

Thinking of Zara laying underneath my brother as he bedded her made me sick.

"Please hurry," I growled as fur rippled along my skin.

I'd only just gotten Zara back, after five years of walking through Hades to be together. I couldn't lose her again.

Madelynn stepped away from the door just as the guard's body hit the floor in front of the cell with a thud. His face was purple and he was ... dead.

"It's done. Now how do we get out of here?"

Wow. She'd taken his life so easily! Without even touching him. "Can you kill my brother from here?" I asked her.

She shook her head. "I could collapse the entire

building but that would kill us too. I need to be closer to him to target my power that precisely."

I nodded, and then tried to think of ways she might be able to pull the door from the cell with her wind power. I'd tried so many things so many times, it was pointless. Iron and stone could hold a man for—

Blue flames burst from the palms of the dragon queen and she glanced over at the rest of us. "Stand back."

We all took several steps back until we were pressed against the far wall. That's when the dragon queen applied the blue flames to the wrought-iron lock.

Hope spurred to life in my chest then. If she could somehow melt the lock and the guard wasn't alive to call for help ... we could really get out of here.

"The second my brother hears us enter the room, he'll use his power," I told the women.

Madelynn looked at me. "I don't need to be in the room with him to take his breath, just outside the room with a small crack under the door will suffice. It will allow me to sense their breathing."

My eyes widened at her words. That was an incredible and terrifying power.

"How will you know whose breath is whose?" I asked. What if she accidently killed Zara?

"I'll know. In that moment, I *am* the wind. It's hard to explain. You're just going to have to trust me."

Trust her. I didn't even know her. I frowned, looking

apprehensively at all of them. How did they get here? Why were they here and not Raife, Drae and Lucien?

The elf queen seemed to read my apprehension and stepped over to me, pulling that tin box from her cloak. I'd seen it when she'd first walked into the dining room and peering at it now was like a blow to the chest. That rusted box wasn't something I ever thought I would see again. It reminded me of a simpler time when I was best friends with the future kings of Avalier.

I remembered the fight my parents got in with my older brother when they chose to send me as the prince to represent us at the yearly retreat with the others. They must have known then that Ansel wouldn't make a good king. He'd always lacked honor. With shaking fingers, I reached out and took the box from her.

"Our husbands said that if we brought you this, it would show you that we are who we say we are, and we *really* need your help."

I nodded, glancing at the dragon queen whose back was now covered in sweat as she continued to blast blue fire at the door. They were all working so hard to free us, to go after Zara and risking their lives when they didn't have to.

Using the edge of my nails, I pulled the lid off. It was stuck and took several tries but when it finally came free, I burst out laughing.

The note on top was in Raife's handwriting.

Princes of Avalier only. Anyone else who open's this will die of rotten diarrhea.

I looked up to see his wife peering over my shoulder, smiling.

"Raife wrote that to scare anyone else off," I told her.

Her smile grew wider then. I was impatient to get to Zara, especially before my brother could hurt her, but it looked like the dragon queen needed more time.

"Almost there!" she announced as if she too had read my mind.

Pulling off the top note, I slipped it into my pocket and then prepared myself for what I would see. This was so long ago. We were little boys, not yet men. We hadn't yet gone through a single trial in life.

I thought the box had been Lucien's idea but I honestly couldn't remember. He'd said he wanted to bury something that made us happy, something we would remember and bring us back to our childhood when we one day became grumpy old kings.

Like we were now.

I glanced down at the contents and smiled at Drae's eagle feather, remembering how much he loved flying. As a wolf I couldn't imagine taking to the skies but it's all Drae spoke about as a child.

Lucien had placed a women's hairclip inside. It was gold with a red painted rose on the tip. It was his mother's, the one person who loved him unconditionally. Lucien struggled with controlling his power and he'd said that his mother was the only one who could bring him back into control. She was his happiness.

My attention then went to the golden arrow tip that Raife had left. I could still remember the sound of his arrows hitting the tree trunks on our yearly retreats. He was never without his bow and took great pride in his skill.

I swallowed hard when I pulled out the seemingly useless ball of wax. It was white and I'd shaped it while still soft. This wax would seem like trash to anyone else, but to me it was one of my greatest memories of my best friends. The candle it came from had burned all night at our yearly retreat that summer, as we stayed up well past our bedtimes and told stories and scared each other and wrestled. That night we'd forged an unbroken bond that neither time nor hardship could tear away. My own brother had been distant and abusive to me so I'd forged a brotherly bond with these boys and rolled all of our memories into this ball of wax to remind me of them.

If any one of them needed me now, I would give them the very clothes on my back.

"Got it!" the dragon queen bellowed, pulling my attention away from the tin box and the emotions they were causing to settle in my chest.

I looked up then to see her booted foot kick the cell door wide open.

I dropped the ball of wax into the tin and snapped the lid shut, looking up at the three women.

"Help me save my mate and I will give you whatever you ask," I told them.

The elf queen nodded. "We ask that you march an army across the realm and fight to defeat the Nightfall queen and liberate our people. Can you do that?"

Go to war. Pull my people from their peaceful lives and march for an issue that did not yet threaten us? I felt the weight of the tin box in my hands and knew that if Raife, Drae and Lucien had sent their wives, it meant they themselves were currently fighting and I would not let them down.

"You have my word."

They looked pleased with that and all nodded once. One by one we left the cell and went in search of Zara. That woman was the strongest I knew, but my brother forcing himself on her was not something I could imagine her enduring. The very thought of it called my wolf to the surface and before I could stop it, I was shifting. Zara Swiftwater was the love of my life. Her laugh had been imprinted on my soul since we were fifteen.

Hold on my love, I'm coming.

Zara

Ansel paraded me down the hall against my will and I tried to scream and thrash, but it was no use. My breathing came out ragged, but nothing more. Halfway down the hall his wife disappeared into another room and I wondered how long his hold on her lasted. Was it based on distance? Or did he merely have to think about her to control her? Were Axil and the queens of Avalier still under his control? It had to exhaust some well of energy within him to use this power, but if it did, he didn't show it. One leg moved in front of the other and no matter how hard I tried to fight it, I walked right into a bedroom with him.

No. No. No.

He closed the door behind me and then spun me around to face him.

"Tell me, did you pine for my brother all those years I had him locked up?" he asked, and I felt my throat loosen. He was allowing me to speak, if I could just keep him talking and not unbuttoning his trousers maybe I could find a way out of this.

"Yes. Since I was fifteen."

Ansel shook his head, looking disappointed. "Love weakens. I tried to teach him that and yet you still ended up together somehow." He removed his tunic, causing my breath to come out in ragged gasps. I was frozen to the spot, unable to move a single muscle except to speak.

"He's my *mate*," I told Ansel. "Love was the only path for us."

Ansel looked at me sharply then, his eyes narrowing. "The Queen Trials aren't about love, they're about strength. They're about marrying the strongest woman of our kind."

Keep him talking, I told myself. *Just keep talking.*

"Can't one have both?" I questioned as he kicked off his shoes. "Love, *and* the strongest woman?"

His eyes went half lidded then and my stomach tied in knots. "I don't think I'm capable of love, but you can sure try."

I opened my mouth to speak again only to find that he'd cut off my words and then I was moving, against my will to the bed.

No.

Reaching down, I grasped the hem of my tunic and pulled upward, stopping halfway as pelts of fur rippled down my arms.

He was undressing me. No. He was forcing me to undress myself. A low rumble sounded in my throat, breaking through his hold on me but then an intense sharp pain sliced through my head and I screamed, reaching up to grab my skull as he allowed.

It was like a hot blade had been stuck inside of my ear and twisted. I panted as the pain came in waves and then just as quickly as it started, it was gone.

My chest heaved as I fought to catch my breath.

Ansel was standing before me in only a loin cloth, grinning. "I like a feisty female," he stated and I saw red.

I lunged forward, breaking his hold for only a few seconds but it was long enough to land a slap on his cheek. Then I was frozen in the air, held in place by his power as he seethed at me.

The skin of his cheek was pink from where I'd hit him, his eyes wide in fury as his pulled his lips back into a grimace.

"I'm going to enjoy putting a pup in your belly," he growled and then stepped forward. I braced myself for his assault, but his face suddenly slipped into panic. Eyes wide, he clawed at his throat while he stared at me in shock.

I was so confused. My slap couldn't have had that kind of effect, right?

He was turning purple.

What in Hades?

A slight wind rushed through the air, picking up my hair like a calling card.

Madelynn was here. This power was unique to the fae queen.

As Ansel's power over me slipped and began to fade away, I slowly regained control over my muscles.

This bastard was going to pay for his treatment of me and the others. I immediately started to shift forms, allowing my head to be the first to turn to beast.

The bedroom door burst open and I didn't even wait to fully shift before I lunged forward. I wanted to be the one to finish him and with the fae queen taking his breath, he was too weak to fight back. I grasped Ansel by the back of the neck with my hands that were shifting to paws and then took his throat into my wolf's mouth. With one clean yank, I ripped it out. Axil had been the first one to burst through the door in his wolf form and now he stood wide-eyed before me and his brother, staring at the scene before him. I spat Ansel's flesh onto the floor in front of Axil's wolf and then Ansel's body hit the ground with a thud. I forced myself back into human form, not fully completing the shift. Then I fell to the ground in front of Axil, pulling his wolf onto my lap.

Axil whined, nuzzling his wolf's snout into my neck.

"I'm okay," I whispered to him.

The three queens were standing in the doorway and looked down at us.

"Are you hurt?" Madelynn asked.

I peered up at her and shook my head.

"Let's give them some time alone," the dragon queen said. "We'll be in the hall."

Then the door closed, it was just me and Axil alone with his brother's corpse. After a full minute of holding him, my heart frantically beating against his wolf, I gently nudged him off and stood. Axil started his shift back into human form and I walked over to a set of drawers at the far wall, throwing clothes on the floor at Axil's feet. I then went into the attached bathroom and washed the blood from my face and mouth, scrubbing my teeth with a brush.

I couldn't believe I'd just killed the wolven king.

Axil's brother.

When I finally came out of the room, Axil was standing before me in low-slung trousers of his brother's that were too short and a tunic that was too tight.

"I ... I'm so sorry," he said.

I walked slowly into his arms and he wrapped them

around me, holding me tightly as the realization of everything that had just happened hit me.

"Did he touch you? Tell me the truth," Axil growled.

I shook my head, peering back to look at him. "No, but if he did would it matter? He's dead."

Axil's blue eyes threaded through with yellow. "Of course it would matter. I'd piss on his corpse and then feed it to a bearin."

I chuckled a little, feeling the mood lighten even if it was in a dark way. "I mean we could still do that. He was a sadistic maniac."

We both turned to stare at the dead purple face of King Ansel, his throat ripped clean out.

"Did you get the power back? Are you king again?" I suddenly looked at Axil. I didn't know how that worked. Before, the brothers had to transfer it to each other through blood. But now ...

Axil nodded but seemed unsettled.

"What's wrong?" I asked. "Are you mad I killed him? I know he was your brother but ..."

He took in a deep breath and then leaned into me, exhaling against my neck which sent shivers along my spine.

"There have to be two living heirs of the royal bloodline otherwise—"

The door burst open and his words were cut off. Axil pulled away and stepped protectively in front of me.

Two red-robed royal wolven advisors were standing in the open doorway and they stared at King Ansel's body in shock.

"Who did this?" the older one with a graying beard asked.

"I did," Axil lied.

My gaze flicked out to the hallway to see the three queens waiting at the ready behind the men.

The advisor sighed. "You should have kept him alive and imprisoned him. Now you'll have to endure the challenge."

The challenge?

Axil shrugged. "He was too dangerous to keep alive."

The advisor nodded as if in agreement. "Well, I will go make an announcement to the pack." Then the advisor looked at me. "Your alpha and friends have been harassing the front guard and inquiring after your whereabouts. I'll let them know you are okay and Axil is back in power."

Wow, I was kind of amazed at how casually they were taking the news that Ansel had just been murdered. But if they'd seen any of what had just transpired over the last twenty-four hours, then they knew and agreed that Ansel was too dangerous to let live.

"What's the challenge?" I asked as one of the advisors left to tell the pack the news but the other stayed. I'm sure Eliza and Cyrus and my little brother were worried but I didn't care about that right now.

The remaining advisor cleared his throat and he held

his head high. "Axil will have to openly fight each pack member who challenges his strength to lead. If there are no longer two heirs of royal blood, then the strongest will lead us."

"Axil is the strongest," I growled, feeling my wolf come to the surface.

Axil reached out and threaded his fingers through mine. "It's okay, love."

But it wasn't. He was still weak and injured from hanging on a hook all day. I looked down at Ansel's body, horrified to find that in my killing him, I'd forced Axil to now have to fight to keep his birthright. I had known about the two-heir thing but hadn't really thought it through or known the repercussions if one died.

"He needs a decent meal and a good night's rest before he fights," I declared to the advisor and dared him to challenge me on that.

He gave me a curt nod. "We will announce that the challenge fights start tomorrow morning."

My heart shattered in that moment. We were so close, so close to our happily ever after. Just as I had to fight to be with him, now he would have to fight to retain his position as king.

The advisor left and the three queens entered the room looking upset by the latest news.

"I'm sorry there will be a delay in our agreement," Axil told the women. "Tomorrow, after I win my place back as king, I promise to uphold my end of the deal and fight alongside you in the war."

The war? The one the queens asked Ansel to help with?

I stared at Axil perplexed and he stroked my palm with his thumb. *'The Nightfall queen is attacking the fae, elvin and dragon-folk as we speak. We will be next if we do not help stop her. They saved you. I owe them everything.'* Hearing his voice in my mind never got old and it was confirmation that he did indeed have his king powers back.

I nodded my agreement and then faced the three women. "Thank you for ..." I looked at Ansel's dead body on the ground, now lying still in a puddle of his own blood.

Madelynn stepped forward. "Of course. We weren't going to let him hurt you."

My heart swelled. These women didn't even know me, and they'd broken Axil out of that dungeon and stolen the very breath from a reigning king's lungs in order to keep me from being defiled.

"Can you stay the night?" I asked them. "We'll have a nice meal prepared for you all. You must be famished from the trip."

Axil and I hadn't eaten and neither had these women. Instead, they'd been thrown in a cell upon their arrival and that was no way to greet visiting royalty. The low growl of a stomach grumbling filled the room and the elf queen giggled. "I could eat."

We all laughed then and the women left the room as

Axil pulled me next to him to follow. Glancing over my shoulder, I looked back one last time at the dead body of Ansel Moon. If they hadn't saved me, that would have been a *really* bad situation.

Now I had other things to worry about. Like my man getting killed tomorrow for fighting to keep his crown.

14

We'd sent someone in to check on Ansel's wife. She was traumatized but happy to be free of his mental control and was promptly returning to Crestline pack territory where she felt most comfortable.

We were almost done with dinner when the doors to the dining hall opened. I'd sent a messenger to bring my brothers, Eliza, and Dorian in to visit.

The moment they entered, I got up and ran to them. Eliza pulled me into a tight hug in which Oslo sandwiched me in by clinging to my back. "We were so worried," she said.

I pulled back and patted Oslo's hair down. He was teary-eyed and couldn't speak.

Cyrus rested a hand on my shoulder. "Glad you are okay."

I nodded.

Dorian was last. He simply looked at me quizzically. "You aged me ten years, child."

I grinned at that and then wrapped my arms around him. He stiffened for a moment but then he rapped my back hard three times and I pulled away.

"Did you hear that—" I started, but Eliza cut me off.

"Ansel is dead and now Axil fights in the morning to retain alpha status?"

"We heard," Dorian said and then looked at the other people in the room.

Right. It was probably big news.

"Guys, this is the elf queen, Kailani, the fae queen, Madelynn, and the dragon queen, Arwen." I introduced my friends and family to the queens we'd had the pleasure of spending the past hour dining with and getting to know.

Everyone joined us at the long table and Dorian cleared his throat, looking at Axil. "My lord, may I speak freely about the challenge tomorrow?"

I stiffened. I didn't want to talk about that, I didn't want Axil to participate in that. But I saw no other way.

Axil nodded. "Of course, Dorian, I respect your counsel."

Dorian had been alpha for a long time, since I was a

little girl, and it was nice of Axil to recognize his seniority and experience.

"From what I've heard around the camp, you'll have five challengers, maybe six."

"Six!" I screeched.

Axil took a slow sip of water and said nothing.

"But the only one you will have to worry about is Brutus," Dorian went on.

"Isn't he Ivanna's alpha?" I asked.

"Yes, he's more beast than man and worse than King Ansel was as far as fairness goes," Dorian told Axil.

Axil inclined his head. "I heard he eats raw bearin heart for breakfast, in his human form, just to make his pack fear him."

Raw bearin heart in human form?

Gross. I loved meat as much as the next wolven but eating the heart raw while in human form was a power play.

"You should fight him first, while you're fresh," Cyrus added but Dorian cut him off.

"That's the thing I wanted to warn you about. Your advisors had them pick sticks: Brutus will be your last fight of the day."

My heart dropped into my gut like a stone and I glanced around the table to see the faces of my friends, new and old alike.

It wasn't good. They were all wearing the same look of pity you wore when someone was dying.

"Can he use his king power?" I knew the answer before I asked.

"No," Dorian said.

Axil looked across the table at my alpha then. "Thanks for the heads up. I'll save my energy for the final fight."

No.

Six alpha challenge fights in one day? There had to be a rule about that. A tear slipped out of my eye and onto the table and I batted it away quickly but Queen Kailani noticed.

She gave a huge fake yawn, stretching her arms above her head. "Boy, am I tired. We should all get some rest."

Madelynn caught onto her train of thought. "So tired." She stood and so did the dragon queen.

Queen Arwen looked down at Axil. "We will stay for the fights tomorrow and then leave to send word back to our husbands with the results."

Yeah, she would stay because she wasn't sure if she would even have a king and his army to help join her war. If Axil died, I doubted Brutus would be inclined to march our people off into uncertainty.

The room cleared out then. My brothers and Eliza gave me one more quick hug before they left and then I found myself alone with Axil for the first time since he'd stepped down as king just to be with me.

How much did he have to love me to do that? My heart suddenly swelled with adoration and I stood, crossing the dining hall until I was before him. He pulled his chair out and I swung my leg over him so that I sat straddling him. His hands came up underneath my tunic to stroke my back and I whispered into his ear, "I can't lose you."

His hands stilled and then I pulled back and peered down at him. There was so much passion in that gaze I felt consumed by it.

"Zara, I've waited *years* to finally have you. I'm not letting anything tear us apart. Even death."

Did it work like that? Would death not claim him because it felt sorry for us? A girl could dream. What Axil needed was someone rooting him on, a woman who stood by him and believed in him.

"Good," I told him, leaning forward and dragging my tongue across his lips. "Because I haven't kissed you enough for you to die yet."

He growled, grasping my butt and standing with me in his arms. Walking over to the edge of the table, he dropped me down onto it. His lips locked with mine and then he consumed me. Every inch of my body was kissed on that table. He threw the dirty food plates to the floor, uncaring about the mess it made. In that moment we allowed love to devour us both, mind, body and soul.

I was Axil's and he was mine. If he died tomorrow, I would have no others after him. There was no point in comparing any man to this one who held me now. They didn't pale in comparison, they vanished.

15

Watching a wolf tear into the man that you loved, while you stood by helpless, was the most gut-wrenching thing I'd ever had to do. Now I knew how Axil must have felt when he'd watched me do the same over the last week. He was on his fifth fight now and though he was winning, he was hurt. I didn't understand why he wasn't allowed to do one fight a day or something more manageable, but I supposed if they wanted the strongest to lead us, this was his way to prove it.

Fight six alphas in one day and live to tell the tale.

The Royal Guard stood in a semi-circle towards the

back of the fight, no doubt wondering who they would be pledging their allegiance to at the end of the day.

Now I stood in almost the same spot as Axil had when he'd watched me fight in the Queen Trials, right next to his empty throne. The queens of Avalier stood beside me as I held on to Eliza's hand in fear and Axil tore into his opponent's neck.

One more fight, I told myself and then glanced over at the giant of a man who would be Axil's last opponent. Brutus was wider than Axil and probably taller too. His arms were riddled with small scars that looked to be from a knife and his head was shaved clean. Brutus stood tall as he watched Axil attempt to end the life of the Copper Canyon alpha.

I steeled myself as Axil took the wolf's neck into his mouth and then a large shadow passed over all of us. Every single person in the crowd craned their neck and tilted their faces upward towards the sky. They pointed to something and then a shadow blotted out the sun.

I spun to see a giant black dragon descending from the clouds. The Royal Guard moved to reach for their bows but the dragon queen rushed forward.

"He's with me," she assured them.

I stared in awe as the large black dragon landed on the open grass with a man sitting in a saddle on his back.

The dragon king was here.

The sound of Axil's whimper drew my attention back to the fight and my head whipped around just in time to see the Cooper Canyon wolf he'd pinned swipe his claw right across Axil's eye, nearly taking it out of the socket.

No!

Axil lunged forward and finished the wolf, ripping his throat out in one clean bite but my heart leapt into my own throat when he looked back at me with one closed eye.

He'd lost his sight in one eye.

No.

No.

No.

It was a death sentence. Especially going up against Brutus next. I looked over at Ivanna's old alpha and he was grinning ear to ear.

"Alright, final fight of the day. Let's do this." Brutus stepped into the ring and I did as well, a growl rising in my throat. He was completely ignoring the fact that a dragon had just landed on the lawn and that Axil had an injured eye. It was a weak move, one I needed to protect my man from.

"The king needs water and to hold council with his training coaches," I called out, stalling for time.

Training coaches? Technically he didn't even have one. But Dorian and Cyrus could pretend to give him tactical advice so that we could check his eye and give him a chance to catch his breath. If we stalled long enough, maybe his eye could naturally heal. Maybe it wasn't that bad. Maybe—

"What's going on here?" a commanding voice boomed from behind me. I'd forgotten about the dragon king. He'd come at the wrong time if he wanted us to roll out the pleasantries.

Dorian and Cyrus moved into the center of the fighting ring to check on Axil while I turned to face Arwen's husband.

He was a mountain of a man, built much more like us wolven than the skinny fae and elvin. He was staring wide-eyed at Axil's bleeding wolf in the center of the fighting ring, clearly shocked to see his old friend, the king, in such a state.

One of the red-robed advisors stepped closer to the dragon king and extended his hand. "King Drae Valdren? You've come at an inopportune time—"

"*What* is going on here?" the dragon king commanded again, holding the stare of the wolven advisor like an alpha would. I liked that he was creating a scene, because it was buying time for Cyrus and Dorian to tend to Axil so I said nothing.

The advisor cleared his throat. "There must be two heirs of royal blood or the king has to enter into a challenge fight with whomever challenges him," he said. "Last night, Ansel Moon was killed and, therefore, King Axil must fight to keep his place as our leader."

Drae looked upset at that news that his old friend was having to fight to keep his birthright and I instantly felt guilty for putting him in that position by killing Ansel. Maybe we should have just locked him up ...

A tall and slender blond male elf stepped up beside the dragon king and rubbed his chin, staring at me. He was the man who'd been riding on the dragon king's back. Kailani wandered over to him and kissed his cheek.

Ahh, the elvin king.

"There *are* two heirs," the elf king stated.

The advisor rolled his eyes. "What do you know, elf? You just got here. Like I said, master Ansel was killed last night, therefore only one wolven carries the Moon bloodline—"

The elf king stepped closer to the advisor and tipped his head up high and his power charged the air, caressing my skin like a tangible thing. "There *are* two if you include the one growing in her belly." He pointed to me and the breath was stolen from my lungs.

"Impossible!" the advisor commanded. "It is forbidden for the king to have any relationship with a candidate in the Queen Trials."

Oops. I was going to have to let that truth come out.

Was this a ruse? He couldn't possibly know I was pregnant this early. *Was* I pregnant? My monthly bleeding wasn't due for over a week and we'd only bedded twice. My heart hammered in my chest like a terrified elkin but hope also grew inside of me. Even if this were a lie, it was a good one. Axil's friend was cunning and this could keep him from having to fight.

"We have bedded since I arrived here last week," I blurted out to the shocked gasps around me. Not exactly queenly behavior but I didn't care – whatever kept this ruse going.

Whatever saved Axil from having to fight Brutus with one eye.

"Lies!" someone from Crestline pack called out. "He's trying to get out of fighting Brutus."

The elf king looked at the man who'd yelled. "I am Raife Lightstone, king of the elves and the greatest healer to ever be known. I can detect life in a woman's belly before even she knows." His voice was strong but held a threat to it.

Chills ran the length of my entire body then. *Was* he telling the truth? Could I really be with child? Tears filled my eyes because I wanted it to be true so badly.

The surrounding wolves gasped and some clapped excitedly. Axil was beloved among his people and I knew they wanted him to carry on his reign if possible.

"Prove you are the elf king! We've never seen you. Otherwise this could be a trick!" someone yelled.

Just when I wondered how in the Maker's name he would do that, Raife nodded, walking over to Axil's wolf.

Axil was lying in a pool of blood with Cyrus and Dorian hovering over him trying to inspect him. There were wounds all over my beloved and it was clear to see his eyeball and lid had been punctured and torn right through.

The elf king kneeled before Axil, and Cyrus and Dorian left to give them space.

Raife looked down at Axil with a grin. "Hello, old friend."

The elf king placed his palm over Axil's eye and a purple light emanated from his hand, causing the entire crowd, myself included, to gasp. King Raife scrunched up his face, squinting his own eye and I wondered if this process somehow hurt him.

We watched in wonder as a moment or two later, the elf king removed his hand and Axil's eye was healed. He blinked up at Raife with a wolfish grin on his face. Raife then left the fighting ring and came to stand by his wife as Dorian whistled to get the crowd's attention.

"We have our proof. There are two heirs! That means Axil is still rightful king!" Dorian shouted.

"No!" Brutus bellowed and lunged for Axil's wolf, shifting in midair. It was the fastest shift I'd ever seen.

I looked at the Royal Guard, who stood at the sides of the ring and were closest to Axil. "Protect your king!" I screamed, running for my mate but I was too far away to stop it.

My heart was in my throat, as Axil bared his teeth, taking the hit of Brutus' wolf head-on. They crashed together snarling and then the Royal Guard pounced. You hadn't seen fighting until you'd seen the ruthless Royal Guard wolves of Death Mountain. They shared one mind as they advanced on Brutus in pack formation. Dirt kicked up, obscuring my vision and the sound of tearing flesh could be heard. Strips of fur and meat were thrown out of the swarming fight and I couldn't take it anymore. I moved to rush deeper into the cloud of dirt when someone grabbed me from behind.

"I got this." Madelynn's voice reached my ear and then a great wind rushed past, pushing the dirt cloud out of the way.

I sighed in relief when I saw that Axil had not moved from where he'd been standing a moment ago. The Royal Guard had torn Brutus to pieces in front of him.

It was over and relief ran through me at the fact that Axil had kept his life and his title as king wolven.

Axil started to shift then, into his human form. Cyrus stepped forward and handed him some trousers and then Axil walked towards me. When our eyes met, my heart exploded because Axil looked at my belly and grinned.

A child.

I peered at the elf king and he nodded, as if telling me this was real, not a farce to save his friend from the challenge fight.

I ran to Axil, stepping over the carnage and not allowing it to dampen this moment for us. We'd made a life together, a life that would be born of our love, carrying with it our struggle to find and finally be with each other.

I crashed into him and his arms came around me and he lifted me into the air, smiling up at me.

"You were worth the wait, my love," he whispered against my lips.

The crowd cheered all around us and I grinned against his mouth, loving that our people were with us.

Someone cleared their throat behind me and Axil set me down as we both turned to face the dragon king.

"I hate to break this up, Axil, but our dear friend Lucien is holding off an entire army by himself and we could really use your help." The dragon king tapped his temple to indicate Axil's gift of being able to control people. I knew it was an invaluable asset in times of war but having just been on the receiving end of it, I wasn't keen on seeing Axil use that power on others any time soon.

Axil sidestepped me and pulled the dragon king into a hug, rapping his back hard twice. "It's good to see you, brother."

Then Raife was there, hugging him as well and all eyes were on my mate. Would he hold up his end of the bargain, would he call our people to war to help his friends?

I hoped so. We owed them everything and Axil was a man of his word.

Axil looked over at his lead Royal Guard. "Ready the troops for war. Half of each household over sixteen must volunteer, man or woman, I don't care."

Chills rushed up my arms. This was happening. I'd never known war in my lifetime but I had heard of the

Nightfall queen's wicked ways. And I had grown to care for Kailani, Madelynn and Arwen. We owed them our life and a war not fought today would eventually find its way to our doorstep tomorrow.

"The Nightfall queen has declared war on all creatures with magic!" Axil bellowed to the amassed crowd. "Let's show her that a wolf cannot be tamed!"

Roars and howls rose up in agreement and then the crowd dispersed to pack up their camps.

When the alpha gave an order, you didn't argue. That was the wolven way.

A woman stepped forward then, not going off to pack up her tent with the rest, and I knew I recognized her from somewhere.

Oh yes. Brutus' wife.

"Zara was going to forfeit. She can't be queen," the woman said.

Everyone froze what they were doing and turned to face the woman. I had to bite back a growl and then stepped closer to her.

"I did that to save a pack sister," I muttered through my teeth at her, and then looked to the crowd, holding up my arms. "Any woman who thinks they are stronger than me, I challenge you right here and now!" I bellowed, my hands balling to fists. I would rip apart any female I had to in order to keep Axil.

A heavy silence descended over the people and I allowed my anger at this woman to rush through me but forced my wolf to stay at bay. I needed to look like I was in control.

To my surprise Eliza stepped into the fight circle and my heart sank into my stomach. There were a few gasps from some of the women watching.

I was more hurt than mad that she would challenge me. Why? "'Liza—" I started, but then she dropped to her knee before me and bowed her head.

Now I understood. She, as the last living champion of the Queen Trials, was sending a message to the other women, and it caused a lump to form in my throat. Amara, from my own pack stepped into the circle next and took the knee as well. Then another, and another, until two dozen women were on their knees before me. Emotion clogged my throat but I swallowed hard and tipped my head up high.

Axil stepped up next to me and then peered at the royal wolven advisors. There were five of them standing there watching the display of submission with female wolves who were anything but submissive.

"What do my advisors say?" Axil asked them and I steeled myself.

They looked at one another, and then one by one nodded.

"Axil Moon remains king and Zara Swiftwater is the people's chosen queen," one of the advisors declared.

The women stood then and Eliza rushed to hug me. I wrapped my arms around her and wished that we could celebrate. Relief and excitement filled me up in equal measure but there was also a sense of foreboding.

The war.

Eliza released me and I pivoted to see that the dragon king and queen were already in their dragon forms with basket saddles on their backs, waiting.

Time was of the essence and celebrations would have to wait.

This was it.

The testing of my capability as queen was at hand.

There was no time for a wedding. I didn't need one anyway. Axil was mine and I was his. I'd been declared queen by the council, there was no need for fancy dresses and dancing. I'd never wanted any of that, I just wanted him. We were accepted by our people, as mates and monarchs, and that's all that mattered to me.

We'd left Axil's lead Royal Guard in charge of the war effort. The wolven troops were set to ride to our aid immediately but we could not wait to travel with them on foot. The fae king needed us now. Axil had spoken of Lucien and his dear friendship and unshakable alliance with the kings of Avalier that summer at camp when we were fifteen. How he went once a year to a retreat to spend time with them and strengthen their bond. Though it seemed like they'd fallen away from each other for some time, it was like no time was lost between them now.

I watched happily as Raife and Axil caught each other up on all they'd missed as we rode atop the dragon king. Next to us, Kailani and Madelynn flew on Arwen's back.

"Married. I never thought I'd see the day," Axil said to Raife over the roaring wind.

Raife smiled. "You don't let a woman like Kailani get away." He looked across the clouds at his wife and I couldn't help but match his smile. I instantly liked Raife: any man who spoke so kindly about his wife was good in my book.

"So, what—" Axil started when a frigid chill slammed into us. Suddenly we were in the center of a snowstorm that had come out of nowhere.

I knew the winter king had a reputation of having an awesome power that he couldn't quite control, and now I was seeing it first-hand.

By my calculations we were still in Archmere, elvin territory, where it did not snow this time of year if ever. Raife looked concerned, his brows knotting together in the center of his forehead. "The war must have gotten worse since we left only a few short hours ago," he said.

The dragon king swooped low, below the thick snowy clouds, and a horrifying sight came into view. Thousands of soldiers, for as far as the eye could see, were attempting to infiltrate Archmere.

There was an ice wall, growing along the border as I looked and blocking the men from advancing across.

Elvin warriors ran to meet them, their arrows sailing over the ice wall and impaling the Nightfall soldiers.

"Get me lower!" Madelynn screamed next to us and Arwen swooped down towards the army of men on the Nightfall side.

Drae followed his wife and then suddenly we were in the thick of the war.

"There's so many," I breathed. Axil reached out and threaded his fingers into mine as we peered at the carnage first-hand. Dead bodies were strewn on either side of the border, Nightfall warriors wore metal glinting contraptions on their wrists and some flung wind and fire like a fae.

Madelynn had told us of the Nightfall queen stealing magical powers but until now, I hadn't seen it for myself.

"No," Axil growled and chills broke out on to my arms. I followed his line of sight and my heart leapt into my throat.

A wolf.

It was smaller than a real wolven and less muscular, and it was running on the Nightfall side.

"They steal our magic but it's not as good or effective for them," Raife told us.

Rage burned brightly inside of me and that's when I

got to witness the full extent of Madelynn's awesome power.

Her battle cry came first, and then a wall of wind slammed into the Nightfall offensive, bodies were tossed into the air like leaves, thrown back hundreds of feet. Trees snapped in half and the very grass was ripped from the earth. She'd cleared the entire border for a hundred yards without harming the ice wall or a single elvin warrior.

"Take that, Zaphira!" she cried from atop Arwen and I looked over at her in awe.

These women, these queens that I now was equal to in status, were awe-inspiring.

"She's amazing," I breathed.

Raife smiled. "Probably more powerful than Lucien, but don't tell him I said that."

We flew over more fighting and carnage, making our way to Thorngate as Madelynn helped to equalize the war from above. But the closer we got to the Nightfall City castle border, the more things looked bleaker on our side. Raife paled beside me as we stared at the bodies of fallen elves and fae alike. It looked like the enemy had somehow gotten over the twenty-foot slick ice wall.

"How did they do that?" I asked, peering over the side of the dragon and then down to see things more closely.

"Some of them can fly and—" The words died in Raife's throat as we all watched a creature on the Nightfall side leap over the barrier with ease and land in Archmere.

Chills rushed up my arms.

No. It couldn't be. They were nearly all wiped out.

The creature ran to the nearest elf warrior at a speed I could barely track and then grasped her by the head, bringing her neck to his mouth. As he drank from her, my fists tightened at my sides.

Necros.

"Maker, help us," Raife breathed. "The necromerians have taken Nightfall's side." His voice was hollow, full of shock.

"No," Axil said and I could hear the astonishment in his voice. "They're neutral. They haven't fought in a war for eons."

It was true they were reclusive outcasts among all Avalierians but as more and more of them soared over the barrier, we realized they were no longer neutral.

The necros were blood-sucking creatures that walked upright like men, and yet could leap a hundred feet into the air and break your back in half with one snap. I hated to admit that fear consumed me then.

I'd never fought a necro before, or seen one, before this moment. Only had I heard stories of their kind: I thought they couldn't go out in sunlight but clearly that was a rumor. A female necro with long black hair looked up at Drae and then crouched. Within seconds she soared into the sky as if she were flying! She launched right at us when Drae belched a stream of fire and then she fell to the ground with a thud.

My heart raced as I took in the entire scene. Turning to Axil with wide eyes, I reached for his hand. "We have to help them."

Innocent elvin people were being slaughtered.

Axil nodded, leaning over the edge of the basket saddle. I knew what he was about to do. I'd never seen him use the king's power and after witnessing Ansel use it wrongly, it made me nervous. But if he could stop those bloodsuckers from killing elvin, I was all for it.

Drae swooped low to the ground and I steeled myself, unsure whether Axil would throw his hands up or shout a command, but no. He just glared at the dozens of advancing necromerians and one by one they stumbled over their feet, then became like rigid soldiers, and I knew he had control over them. They marched without anima-tion over to the nearest weapon or sharp object and impaled themselves upon it. I winced at the sight but I also approved.

This was war and when you were at war, it was a case of anything goes.

Raife clasped Axil on the back in gratitude and Axil nodded. It was one of the darkest things I'd ever seen. To make someone end their own life ... but they'd chosen their side and we had to see it through now. Until the end.

After taking care of the necromerians, Drae flew us higher and into Thorngate where the temperature plunged. Thick chunks of snow fell from the sky as I pulled my furs tighter around me.

In no time at all we were landing before a giant white castle, blanketed in snow.

This was the famed Winter Court.

Madelynn leapt off of Arwen and bolted inside, seemingly in search of her husband. I followed Raife who led Axil and I past front steps filled with soldiers, and inside.

The moment we crossed the threshold, I was blasted with the warmth of a fire, and was grateful for it. Madelynn was there hugging a handsome-looking very tall fae with ink-black hair. They pulled away when they saw us and Lucien Thorne took one look at Axil and me, and grinned. "You came."

I wasn't sure if I were imagining it but the pupils in Lucien's eyes looked clouded like snow. Whatever storm was happening outside, he was somehow controlling it in here.

Axil stepped forward and embraced his friend. "Of course I came: you sent the box. I had no choice."

Lucien chuckled and by now Arwen, Drae and Kailani had joined us.

"The necromerians have joined the fight?" Raife said beside us.

Lucien looked stressed, reaching up to rub at his temples. "Right after you flew away, we got the first wave of them. Didn't understand what I was seeing for a second."

The dragon king let out a low whistle. "I wonder how Zaphira got the necros to agree to fight against us."

"Who cares: how do we defeat them?" Arwen asked and went to stand next to her husband.

Everyone turned to look at Axil, myself included.

"Can you control them all?" Lucien asked.

Axil shook his head. "An entire army? I'm not sure my mind can do that alone."

"I understand," Lucien said but he appeared distraught.

"Alone?" I asked, noticing that Axil had used specific wording.

He stared warily at me, almost as if he didn't want me to pick up on that. "I could, for a short period of time, share the king's power with another dominant wolf."

Another dominant wolf. Me.

"Let's do it," I said immediately.

He shook his head. "What if you get hurt or ..." He peered at my stomach. I had wanted to pull Raife aside and ask if it was really true, if I was really pregnant but I didn't have a chance. Maybe it was all just a ruse.

"I'm strong, you said so yourself, and any child we make will be the same," I told him.

He sighed and then inclined his head. "Are you sure you can handle this?"

"Completely sure."

Raife rubbed his hands together in excitement. "If you can share the burden of holding back the necros, it could save thousands of lives. Just long enough for us to break through and kill the queen." He looked at Axil hopefully.

Axil glanced at me again as if he needed more confirmation that I truly desired to do this. I reached out and squeezed his hand, an idea forming in my mind. "I'll bet we could get some horse saddles modified to fit on our wolven backs." We were smaller than horses but not by much.

Lucien's eyes lit up. "What are you suggesting?"

I gave everyone in our little meeting a sly grin. "Axil and I ride as a team with one of you on our wolven backs. We use our power to hold off any attacks and walk you right into the queen's inner camp."

Drae gasped slightly. "It's brilliant. Yes! And Arwen and I can circle above trying to keep any air assault away from you."

"I want to do it," Raife said suddenly and everyone turned to look at him.

"Do what?" Lucien asked his friend.

The normally peaceful healer fisted his hands. "I want to be the one to slit her throat and whisper the names of my family in her ear before she burns in Hades."

Whoa. It was a well-known rumor that the Nightfall queen had taken out his entire family, though it was one I hadn't believed until right now.

Axil placed a hand on Raife's shoulder and squeezed. "You can ride with me."

"I'll manage the troops at the front line with Madelynn. Freeze anyone who gets through," Lucien said.

Madelynn nodded, stepping up next to her husband.

"And I will ride on Zara," Kailani said and peered over at me. "If that's okay? I know the Nightfall realm the best. I grew up there," she added, a little shamefacedly.

I gave her an easy smile. "That's perfect." I'd given wolf-back rides to Oslo and his friends all the time, sometimes three of them at once. My wolf was ten times stronger than I was. I'd be slower than normal but that was okay: it was my mental acuity that would need to be up to the task if I were going to ... control people against their will.

A nursemaid suddenly came over then holding two infants, one in each arm and I gasped.

They were so perfect and tiny.

With bright grins, Drae and Arwen each reached for a baby and pulled them to their chests, peppering their faces with kisses.

"They're adorable," I told Arwen and she looked up at me beaming. Twins were common in wolven births too. Sometimes triplets.

It made me think of the life growing inside of me and whether that had been one hundred percent true or not.

"Raife, can I speak to you for a minute?" I inclined my head to a spot a few steps away by the roaring fire.

He nodded and followed me.

Once he was standing before me, I grasped my flat stomach. "Am I *really* with child? I won't be mad if that was a trick because it saved Axil's life."

He beamed at me. "You are. It's very early but I see it

as a small flicker of golden light in your womb." He glanced at my stomach and I couldn't believe how incredible his healing gift was to detect life even before a mother could. "And I don't think using any mental gifts will interfere with the pregnancy at this stage."

Tears lined my eyes but I blinked them back. "Thank you," I told him and we walked back over to join the others. I knew with Axil's sensitive hearing and the fact that we hadn't stepped too far away that he'd probably heard. When I stepped back up beside him, he ran a hand over my belly and grinned at me. "Okay, I'm going to need some time to train Zara," he said.

Lucien looked like he was mentally half here, and half with the storm outside. "When will your wolves be here?" he asked dreamily.

"It might take two days or more with such a large contingent but I can have a smaller elite force here within hours if Arwen and Drae are willing to fly them," Axil said, peering at the dragon king and queen.

The husband and wife shared a glance and then nodded. "We can fly runs all night, holding two to four people each until we have enough."

That was a relief. If they could get the Royal Guard here then the necromerians didn't stand a chance.

Raife cleared his throat. "I appreciate that you've called your entire army for us, Axil, but if your power is great enough, we may not need them. We can end this tomorrow morning."

"No pressure." Axil laughed nervously.

Raife clapped his dear friend on the back. "I saw what you did back there with the necros. It was incredible. We just need that on a larger scale."

Axil turned to face me. "Then if you'll excuse us, Zara needs to train."

We walked out of the living room and into a small library. It was cute that Axil seemed to know where he was going, which meant he'd been here before. Probably as a kid.

Axil looked around, seemingly stuck in his memories and then glanced at me. "You know what it feels like to pull on your dominant power and hold another dominant's gaze?"

I nodded. As a female in a pack of strong males I'd had to do it often.

"Well, controlling another person against their will is a lot like that. But instead of holding eye contact you ..." His lips thinned as he stared off into the rows of books in the distance, seemingly at a loss for words. "You hold the image in your mind of what you want them to do and ... *push* it over them. You wrap them in it until they are forced to do it," he finished and then shook his head. "I'm sorry I've never had to explain this to another person before. My father taught Ansel and I when we were younger."

I nodded. "That's okay. I think I know what you mean.

It's like holding a thought in your head of a person kneeling, and they kneel?"

"Sort of, yeah. Do you want to try it on me first?"

My eyes widened. Control Axil? Against his will? The thought felt so wrong and yet I knew he was the best person to practice with.

"Uh, sure," I said hesitantly.

"You won't hurt me," he said, and then placed his arm over mine. "Hold my gaze."

I had friends who were submissives and they said it was uncomfortable to hold a dominant's gaze, that when they locked eyes with their alpha for too long, their insides churned.

Not me. It gave me a thrill. My heart would pound in anticipation of how long I would be able to hold it.

"I'll have to bring you into Death Mountain pack," he stated.

Even though I knew that was inevitable, my heart pinched a little at the thought of leaving Dorian, Amara, my brothers ... Eliza. They wouldn't be pack family anymore. But Axil was my family now, and so was this child in my belly and I'd have to join Death Mountain pack to truly be queen of the wolven.

"Okay." I handed him my wrist upturned.

I locked eyes with Axil fiercely, gritting my jaw as he dragged a clawed finger down my arm and drew blood. The dominance of the alpha king was unlike anything I could describe to an outsider. Looking at Axil now, there was a knowing that he could take me in a fight, that he could take over my will, but also that he would protect me at all costs, that I could depend on him for anything. That's what true dominance was in a wolf pack. My leader, my protector, my mate.

I gasped when he pressed his bloody wrist to mine.

"Zara Moon ..." He gave me his last name and I had to suppress a whimper of surprise. It felt so right. "I claim you for Death Mountain pack and I share this burden with you. The magic of my forefathers."

I gasped as I felt a literal tearing away from my brother, Dorian, Eliza, everyone in the Mud Flats. It was like a constant knowledge in the back of your mind that someone was there and now they were suddenly gone. It was replaced with new people, Axil and all of the Death Mountain wolves. Then I felt his magic, and I wasn't prepared for the hot buzzing sensation to crawl up my veins and into my chest. I shuddered as the magic completely entered me and settled just under my skin.

"You feel it?"

I swallowed hard and nodded. It was an unnerving thing, like you were sharing your body with someone else. My wolf was there, and one other. This magic.

I realized then that I'd been holding his gaze the entire time without issue. "You'll be more dominant while you carry the power," he told me and then stepped five paces away from me, putting his hands at his sides. "Now make me kneel."

I swallowed hard, trying to concentrate.

"Kneel!" I shouted with force, but nothing happened.

Axil shook his head. "You don't have to say it. Ansel did that for theatrics. Focus on the vision of my kneeling and then wrap it in the magic and ... *throw* it at me."

Right.

Closing my eyes, I envisioned the king of the wolven bowing his head and dropping to one knee before me. I felt the magic stir to life inside of me and I opened my eyes and pushed that vision over him as if I were throwing a fishing net and capturing him in it.

He winced for a second and then dropped to one knee, head bowed.

I gasped, releasing the hold I had over him and he looked up at me with a grin.

"You're a natural."

My heart pounded as the power coursed through me. "You've had this the whole time?" I asked him, looking at my hands as if they were weapons.

He nodded. "The burden of a wolven king. Knowing when to use it and when to refrain. Something my brother never learned." He growled that last part.

"How do you use this on multiple people?" I asked, thinking of the impending army of blood drinking necromerians we were about to attack.

He sighed, stepping closer to me. "Very skillfully." He reached out and traced the side of my cheek. "Most men would want to tuck their woman away and hide her from harm, but I know how strong you are," he told me, eyes blazing yellow. "I know that we can win this war, together."

His confidence in my abilities made me smile.

"With that being said ..."

I steeled myself for him to tell me to stay home because I was fragile, or pregnant, or both.

"How about I worry about subduing the masses, and you just make a path through it all so we can get Raife to the queen."

He didn't want me to take on too much stress and I understood that.

I dipped my chin indicating I understood and agreed. "No offense to the elf king, but isn't he a healer and not a fighter?"

I hated to question his dear friend but was this man going to be able to kill the famed Nightfall queen, Zaphira?

Axil gave me a wolfish grin. "Raife could split an arrow from a mile away."

Okay, clearly I had misjudged the great healer and had completely forgotten about the famed elvin Bow Men.

"But without his bow?" I asked; I hated to admit I had a bit of a prejudice thinking that the elves were weak warriors compared to the dragon-folk or fae.

Axil placed both hands on my shoulders. "The Nightfall queen killed his entire family. Poisoned them in front of him. Nothing burns brighter than the hatred he has of this woman. He will remove her heart from her chest with his bare fingers if he has to."

I nodded with approval. Now that sounded like my kind of warrior.

"Then I'm ready. Let's do this." I stood tall and proud. I wanted Axil to know that I was with him, as his mate, his queen, no matter what.

He chuckled. "Easy there. Let's practice a bit more first."

FOUR HOURS LATER, after a large dinner and nearing 2 a.m., I had all the kings and queens of Avalier bowing before me in the drawing room. I'd been practicing for over two hours and Arwen and Drae had just got back from their second run. We now had a dozen of the elite wolven guard getting up to speed on the war with Lucien's commander.

"This is fun," I said.

"Okay, I think she has mastered the skill, Axil, my knees hurt," Arwen griped jokingly and I released my hold over them all.

One by one they stood and appraised me.

"This will work," Raife said excitedly. "If she can just get me within bow range of the queen, we end this."

Lucien and Madelynn were mentally absent, but

physically present using their powers to control the weather outside.

"There's more of them," Madelynn said in an eerie voice. "The necros. We should attack soon, at first daylight, for I fear if we let them amass ..." Her voice trailed off.

Lucien nodded his agreement, his eyes looking far off into the room. "It's now or never. We get a few hours' sleep and then prepare to leave." He motioned to me and Axil.

I'd always been fascinated by the power the fae held. To be able to control nature itself was incredible.

"My men are being briefed on the situation: I'll let them know we ride at first light," Axil told them.

I peered over at Raife and was alarmed to see him grinning.

Kailani cleared her throat. "Darling ... what's so funny?"

He shook himself, wiping the smile off his face. "Oh nothing, I just thought of the queen dying and gasping for air and got excited. I don't think I'll be able to sleep."

Kailani peered at all of us with wide eyes and reached out to pat his shoulder. "Let's keep creepy thoughts to ourselves, darling."

We all burst into laughter at that. Raife was probably the only one in the room who was excited for morning.

17

I'd barely slept, only about two hours, but it was enough. After finishing our breakfast while the sky was still dark, we made our way to the stables.

The maker of the saddles that had been used on the dragon king and queen was able to retrofit a couple horse saddles for Axil and me. We'd finalized the plan and it was decided that Axil would carry Raife on his back and I would carry Kailani. Meanwhile, Arwen and Drae would take to the skies, watching over us from above and Madelynn would stay on the ground, using her wind to blow back any assault on the Winter Castle where her little sister and Arwen and Drae's twins were being kept safe.

Surrounding us would be the armies of Avalier mixed with dragon-folk, elves and fae. And our elite royal wolven army. If the war went on for days, then the wolven would arrive and bring an even stronger show of force. Ten thousand strong all together with the others. The necromeres were a surprise but nothing we couldn't handle together. I was feeling good about things.

It was a great plan, nearly a perfect plan if everything went accordingly.

I turned to look at Axil and ask him something when I saw the color drain from his face. I frowned as he stared far off into space, seemingly lost in his thoughts.

"Axil?"

His gaze snapped to mine and he swallowed hard. We were in the stall of a barn, about to shift and have our saddles put on. He crossed the barn and reached for my face with shaky hands. "My love, one of my advisors has given me grave news." His voice cracked and something inside of me broke.

It was bad. Whatever it was, was so bad. Axil had a constant mental link to his advisors, it was part of his alpha magic. It meant that no matter the distance, or form, they could communicate.

By the look on his face, his advisor had just told Axil something truly awful.

"No," I whimpered, not wanting to know whatever it was that had made Axil look as if he'd seen death.

Tears filled his eyes and his bottom lip quivered. "Last night, Queen Zaphira sent an army of necromerian raiders to Fallenmoore. She must have been watching—"

"Axil, tell me!" I screamed, a sob already forming in my throat.

He released a shaky breath and looked me right in the eyes, his own still welling with tears. "Cyrus was killed and Oslo was taken."

Nothing in this world could have prepared me for those words to come out of his mouth. My legs collapsed beneath me and everything went dark.

I CAME to in Axil's arms a few moments later. Raife was there, some purple light glowing from his palm to my face as I blinked rapidly.

Why was I lying on the floor of the barn? Pure grief poured through me at the memory of what Axil had told me.

I sobbed and rolled onto my side as my wolf took over. I couldn't be strong, not in my human form, it was too much to bear.

Cyrus. My sweet big brother. My coach. A husband. Father.

No. This couldn't be happening.

But it was.

I welcomed the pain that the snapping of bones and ripping of muscles brought. It felt good in this moment. I wanted to feel hurt, it was better than feeling hollow. Like a huge gaping hole had opened in my chest.

Tipping my head up, I let loose with a gut-wrenching howl. I couldn't help but wonder if Axil hadn't claimed me last night if I would have felt Cyrus dying through the pack link. Something strong like that, a death, could be felt by all pack members. Maybe it was a small mercy I didn't.

I expected Axil to take me into his arms, to try and sooth me with words but instead it was Raife who knelt before me, grasped the sides of my wolf's face lightly and forced me to look into his gaze.

"I know," he said calmly, eyes glowing with rage. "I *hate* that I know exactly how you feel but I do. Zaphira took my mother, father and all of my siblings from me in one fell swoop and I've waited *years* for this revenge."

My wolf whimpered as I held his stare and I felt in that moment that he was the only one in the world who understood me and what I was going through.

"But you don't have to wait years for your revenge, Zara," he said. "You can get it now and you can save your little brother before she takes him too."

Oslo. At the mention of his name, I sprang into a standing position, forcing Raife to let go of my face. The only thing that parted the dark clouds of my grief was the thought of my little brother.

"Ready?" Raife asked.

I nodded eagerly. If the Nightfall queen did have Oslo, she was about to learn that she'd messed with the wrong woman.

Just then the barn doors were thrown open and Kailani ran inside, panting. "I heard about your little brother getting taken. I know where the queen would hide him, and how to get into the castle."

This had just become a rescue mission.

I looked up at Axil and he appeared conflicted for a moment. This changed everything, Oslo was taken – we had to save him first.

"Let's do it," Axil agreed.

Kailani rushed forward, making quick work of strapping the saddles to our backs. If she grew up in Nightfall City and knew the area like the back of her hand, then I needed her to get Oslo back. If we were to infiltrate the castle, she was our best bet.

"Where are your clothes for after you shift?" Kailani asked and I indicated to the pile of clothing in the corner. She scooped it up, stashed it in her bag and then leapt onto my back without fear.

I looked over at Axil, and he spoke into my mind using our newly formed pack link. *'We'll be able to communicate in wolf form. Leave the dangerous stuff to me and Raife, and you just worry about getting Oslo free.'*

I dipped my head. *'I will.'*

With that, we stepped out of the barn and onto the

snowy ground. Our small contingent of Royal Wolven Guards was waiting for us in a V pack formation. Axil nodded to them as he passed and they fell into line behind us. I tried not to allow my mind to wonder what I could have done differently to save Cyrus. Arwen and Drae had made so many runs last night getting the Royal Guard here, it was almost like the necromerians had waited until they were done before they attacked. The calculated ruthlessness of it made a flame of rage burn within me.

It had been snowing for hours and there was a permanent chill in the air which was to be expected in the Winter portion of the fae realm. I had thick wolf fur and the Mud Flats often got snow, so it didn't bother me. The only thing on my mind was my little brother. I'd lost my parents, now Cyrus, I couldn't lose him too.

It was about an hour's sprint to the border. The fae, elvin and dragon peoples had done a wonderful job of coming together to amass a united front against the Nightfall army. I saw fae standing beside elvin folk and everyone working together. It was a beautiful thing given the circumstances, and I was proud our people were on their way to lend a hand.

Kailani was holding on to the saddle tightly so I rode fast and hard with Axil and Raife right beside us. When we reached the ice wall at the border, I steeled myself.

The necromerians were sailing over the wall only to be skewered by the elvin Bow Men.

THE FORBIDDEN WOLF KING

'How are we going to do this?' I asked Axil, suddenly feeling overwhelmed.

There were people dying left and right and blood-sucking necromerians stood in our way. I would have said that flying by air would be the best option but as I looked up, I saw the glint of metal wings. Their skies were littered with them. The Nightfall queen and her machines seemed to have no end to what they were capable of.

'The Royal Guard and I will carve a path for you,' Axil said and I trusted him enough to take him at his word. I had to think about my brother now, everything else was secondary.

Hold on, Oslo, I thought. If that madwoman hurt a hair on his head, I would skin her alive and all of her children too. I could not be trusted to remain reasonable where my family was concerned. If you harmed those I loved then all honor was dead and I wasn't going to play by the rules. This was my game now and I intended to win. By the end of this day, I would either lie dead on the ground or the queen's head would be stuck to a spike in the center of Nightfall City.

Nothing in between.

With a growl, I took off running and Axil followed. We gained speed and then, as if sharing one mind, we leapt up and over the giant ice wall together and landed in the center of the chaos below. The Royal Guard jumped high over the wall as well and settled at our side, fanning out to flank us.

The Nightfall warriors and the necromerians immediately turned their attention to us and I steeled myself.

But nothing happened.

They stood frozen like marble statues and I knew in that moment that Axil was controlling them.

"Now!" Raife cried, and a barrage of arrows rained down from the trees, piercing the frozen warriors in the chest. Our Royal Guard leapt from their positions and ripped out the throats of the necros.

It all was happening so fast I couldn't process it.

"Go!" Kailani lightly kicked me with her heels, like you would a horse, and that got me moving. I bolted from the crowded space and through the woods, towards the center of their lands and where Nightfall City castle lay beyond. A great wind rushed past us and I assumed it was Madelynn for a second until I saw a human male with short-cropped ears running towards us with his arms outstretched.

He had wind power!

I remained calm, pulling on the wolven king's power that Axil had shared with me and imagining the man freezing to the spot, his knees going stiff. Then I threw the power over him. Suddenly he tripped over his feet and then lay on the ground, stiff as a fallen log.

Good enough.

I pressed on, trying to remain out of sight, darting through the trees in the direction Kailani gently coaxed me in. As I was barreling through the woods, freezing one or two warriors in our way, we suddenly came upon a cluster of necromerians. They were standing around a map talking battle strategy as I burst from a thicket and right into their midst.

There were over a dozen of them and they leapt backwards, startled, a few of them hissing. I skidded to a stop before them and Kailani let a curse word fly. I felt that king's power course through my veins but before I could even concentrate to use it, the necros pounced.

They were so fast. I blinked and then they were on us.

My first fear was Kailani. I had no idea of her abilities and so I darted to the side to avoid two of the bloodsuckers but took a third head-on. It leapt onto my back, right where Kailani was riding and I steeled myself. A fourth came for me and I tore into her leg with my jaws. A body flew from my back, landing before me, and I was relieved to see it wasn't the elvin queen. A dagger lay embedded in the chest of the necro.

Freeze, I thought and pushed it out like a net. The necros slowed but didn't stop.

I remembered Axil's advice. It was less about the word and more about the vision of it. Which was impossible to do when panicking! I imagined all of the necros suddenly grasping their heads in horrific pain, and one by one they dropped to their knees screaming.

I gasped, feeling like I'd done some dark thing, but again Kailani clicked her heels.

"Go!" she urged.

I ran, but the sick feeling that I was no better than Ansel stuck with me. Why did I feel bad for causing pain to someone who was trying to kill me? It was the dominant in me. It just felt wrong to control someone else like that, though it was needed in this moment. Axil was right, it was more of a burden than a blessing.

I went slower this time, creeping through the woods and watching for clusters of Nightfall warriors. I could see the castle looming on the horizon and with renewed strength, I ran harder.

"Near the west wall there is a storm drain, we will cross into the city that way if we can," Kailani told me.

It was early morning. I feared we would be seen and killed by an arrow but kept that to myself. Best to assess the situation when we got there. I slowly made my way in that direction, only stopping when I heard a twig snap behind me.

'It's me.' Axil's voice came into my mind before I saw him. He ran up alongside me with Raife still firmly on his back. Both were covered in dirt and blood and wore signs of battle but otherwise seemed okay.

'The Royal Guard?' I asked him, relieved he wasn't hurt.

'They are helping on the front lines. I'm going to get Raife inside and hopefully he can assassinate her and be done with this before too many more people have to die.'

Raife looked at his wife. "Storm drain?"

"If we can," she responded.

With that we moved our way through the woods, keeping watch for more warriors making their way to the front lines. The entire war seemed to be amassing along the border of Thorngate and Archmere.

There were a few sparse necros or Nightfall soldiers here and there but nothing we couldn't handle. When we finally made it to the west side of the wall that surrounded Nightfall City, my heart sank into my stomach.

There were over fifty men pacing along the top, bows in hand as they readied themselves to defend their home. There was no way we could get past all of them. Could Axil force his will upon that many? Probably ... but for how long? And if even one person raised the alarm, there were more inside, surely? We hid behind a cluster of bushes, all silent and lost in our own thoughts.

Kailani stepped off me and started to unhook my saddle.

I looked at her, perplexed, but she turned to address her husband. "We need a distraction. Draw the men to the north side of the wall so that Zara and I can slip inside."

Okay, that was smart. Her ideas were good.

'I can do that. Take Raife in case you see the queen. Just end this,' Axil said for my ears only, but I felt anxious at the idea of him taking this risk for me, for Oslo. What if they killed him?

"I need you human to fit in the storm drain." Kailani looked down at me and placed the stack of clothes at my front paws.

'Axil, what if you get hurt?' I peered at him, trying not to let the fear leak across our bond.

He looked over at me with blazing blue eyes. 'What if they are hurting Oslo right now?'

That statement caused a whimper to form in my throat.

'I can't live with that, Zara,' Axil said. 'He is of you, and therefore he is of me. Go get him and I will take care of things out here.'

I padded forward, out of the heavy saddle and nuzzled his neck with my snout. 'I love you,' I whimpered. 'Now. Forever. Always.'

We stayed like that for a moment, Raife and Kailani giving us our time to say goodbye. The importance of what he had said pressed upon me then; Oslo could be getting hurt right this moment. When I felt I had said a proper farewell, I started my shift. After changing quickly, I crouched in my human form and kissed the top of Axil's wolf head.

Then I stood, careful to remain behind the bushes and walked up to Raife. He held my gaze, having no idea what Axil and I had said to each other.

"Axil will cause the distraction alone. You come with us and if we find the queen, we finish her. End this war."

Raife grinned in approval but then the smile slipped from his face as he glanced at his old friend. One man taking on fifty warriors was not a fair fight.

The sound of crunching leaves pulled my attention to

the right and I reached for my knife but stopped when I saw the shock of red hair.

Madelynn jumped into our little hidden bush alcove and gave Axil a lopsided grin. "Need some help? I've always wanted to ride on a wolf."

Relief rushed through me and I pulled her into a hug, crushing her tightly in my arms.

"Thank you," I whispered. I barely knew this woman but she was a very powerful fae, and alongside Axil, she might just be the only person able to help him fight that many men and keep him alive.

She squeezed me back and nodded.

Without further fanfare she leapt onto the saddle atop Axil's back and then looked over at Kailani, Raife and me. "I heard it was going to be windy today." She winked and then Axil took off, darting out into the open as a giant wind tunnel appeared in the field above the northern end of the gate.

"I love her," Kailani said.

"Me too," I added.

Raife went very still then, taking in a deep breath and pulling an arrow from his quiver. He nocked it and then looked at us. "The Nightfall queen is inside these walls. I can sense it. And I will not leave without the tip of this arrow embedded in her heart."

It was time to seek revenge. When Zaphira took my little brother, she had no idea who she was dealing with.

The commotion that Madelynn and Axil made at the north end of the wall allowed us to slip into the storm drain and pop out inside the city undetected. I had no pointed ears to hide, neither did Kailani, so it was just Raife who had to keep his long white hair and sharp tipped ears disguised under a hat while we were inside the human city.

There were shouts of alarm along the upper castle wall and the residents were running about quickly, closing up shops as warriors mounted horses for war. We mimicked their frantic movements, rushing through town towards an industrial area.

"What is the extent of your powers now?" Kailani whispered. "Can you make someone unlock a door or give us keys?"

Panic washed over me at the thought that getting my brother back might hinge on my using a power that I had held for a grand total of one day. "Doubtful, but I could freeze them until you stole the key," I told her honestly.

She nodded. "That would work."

"You think the queen is experimenting on him?" Raife asked his wife as we jogged towards the giant buildings. But his words made me stumble and I had to steady myself as I followed them, worried what Kailani's answer would be.

"I do. I think she wants his wolf magic," she stated and that caused my panic to increase. "Or she knows he is the new wolf queen's brother, and wants him as a hostage. In which case he would be in the dungeon."

Okay, that was even more terrifying.

We kept our heads down and weaved in and out of the streets until we stood before a large brick building with giant glass windows. There were two guards patrolling the front, each holding a harpoon spear type of weapon that glinted in the light.

Kailani looked to me. "Show time."

I steeled myself as she walked right through the gates and up to the men. They gripped their weapons, raising them slightly as she approached and I concentrated on freezing them from further movement. I envisioned them frozen like statues and then used the king's magic to throw it over them. Their limbs ceased moving, but they were also unable to speak.

Kailani looked left and right at the passing people and reached into one of the guards' waist belts from where she produced a set of keys.

Slipping them into her pocket, she looked back at me. "Make them walk to the side of the building with us."

Walk them! I wasn't sure I could do that. Already I could feel them fighting me. It was like someone pushing back at me physically. Holding on to the power, I envisioned them walking forward and both of the guards lurched onward, knocking into Kailani and causing her to yelp.

A few people glanced in our direction and we smiled nervously. The guards looked like they had sticks up their butts, walking in a jerky abnormal pattern.

Raife rushed to the side of one guard and linked his arms through to steady him and Kailani did the same with the other. This did not look natural and any passersby would think they were drunk.

"Sorry," I whispered as we all made our way away from the front of the building to the side where there was no one watching. We were shaded by the structure now and completely hidden by the fence.

The guards' eyes were wide and I felt slightly bad that

I was controlling them this way, but knowing they could be guarding a building my brother was in, I got over that guilt quickly.

Kailani looked at me and then cracked one of the guards over the head with a small rock she'd been hiding behind her back. He crumpled to the ground and then she repeated the action with the next one. Raife appraised his wife with pride and then they both made quick work of tying the guards' hands behind their backs.

"Okay, we don't have much time. Let's check inside and if Oslo's not there ... they will have him in the dungeon," Kailani said.

I frowned. "The raid just happened last night: what if they are still traveling back on foot?"

Axil got the news just after it happened and Fallenmoore was at least a day's journey on foot—

"They have flyers. Humans with metal wings. I'm sure they flew him here as he's a high-value target," she said and I swallowed hard, not wanting to believe they already had my little brother and might be experimenting on him.

Keys in hand, Kailani ran for the side door and unlocked it. She seemed like she knew her way around this building and I was grateful. Raife and I slipped inside after her and I noticed we were in an open hallway lined with closed doors. The elf queen ducked into a room to the right and emerged wearing a white coat.

"Head down, patient," she told me and handed Raife the other coat and a clipboard.

Oh. Right. I would act like a patient in this ... whatever it was. A place they stole our magic? The thought gave me the shivers, but it was good thinking if we were caught.

I heard a few voices up ahead and Kailani hooked her hand under my elbow as I held my arms behind my back in a mock cuffed fashion. Then she marched us forward with confidence. This woman was full of more courage than I'd given her credit for when I'd first met her. I'd mistaken her kindness as a submissive weakness. I was wrong. And I was so grateful she was here with me now because I was feeling anything but confident.

We entered a main room where two others in lab coats were making hot tea and chatting easily. Kailani walked past them and they barely glanced in our direction. Only when we entered another hallway did one of them call after us.

"Hey, where are you taking that patient?" the woman questioned.

Kailani froze, not looking back. "Do you know which room Oslo Swiftwater is in? The little wolf boy from Fallenmoore?" she asked over her shoulder.

My heart hammered in my chest at her bold question.

"Who?" the woman in the lab coat called out. "We don't have any wolves right now."

That was a relief and also a worry. Where was he?

"Hey, who are you?" the woman demanded and I spun round, throwing my magic over her and her male counterpart and freezing them both mid stride.

"He's not here," I whined as Raife and Kailani subdued and tied up the two physicians.

Kailani looked worried. "Then there is only one other place he would be. I have to get you into the castle."

She motioned that we head back the way we came and my heart fell. I wanted him to be here. I wanted this to be easy.

We stepped outside to where the two unconscious guards were. Kailani stripped down to her undergarments and put on the guard's uniform. Raife did as well, tucking his hair into a bun and shoving it deep into his hat.

"What's your plan, my love?" he asked her, strapping his bow over his back.

She looked up at him. "We arrest her, bring her in and say we have captured the wolf queen."

Raife's face fell. "They could kill her. Or strip her magic."

Kailani swallowed. "I know, but it's the only way I know how to get her inside. The palace is heavily guarded, we will be lucky if we are not recognized and caught while handing her over."

"Do it," I commanded. I didn't care what happened to me, I just needed to be with my brother.

Raife turned to face me. "You have the king's power right now. If Zaphira puts you in one of her machines, then she will have it too. She could control everyone. We can't let that happen."

I nodded. "If she brings me towards any machine, I

will turn my fingers to claws and cut my own throat out before I give her my magic. I swear it." Kailani looked horrified at my suggestion but Raife nodded as if he were pleased with that answer. I knew the cost of what I carried and that it could never fall into enemy hands. I just prayed it wouldn't come to that.

"I'll find my way into the castle and protect you," Raife told me but I knew it was an empty promise. No one could give me such an assurance but I appreciated it nonetheless. My mind wandered to what Axil and Madelynn were doing right now. Had they retreated? Were they hurt? Had they come inside the city walls to look for us? That would be crazy. I just hoped they were alive.

Kailani shook her head. "For all the work we did to bring the kingdom together in the war, I can't believe it's up to just the three of us to do this."

Raife nodded. "It was always going to be me that killed her." Reaching into his pocket, he pulled out a small clear vial and I frowned.

"Colorless, odorless poison. I have dreamed about Zaphira choking on it since I was fourteen."

Wow, that was dark, and yet I totally approved. "If she's in there, go for it. Don't worry about me," I told him. "I'll get my brother out."

Kailani pulled me in for a hug and then kissed her husband chastely. We all knew the likelihood of us surviving this was not great.

"Okay, Zara gets Oslo out, Raife tries to kill the queen,

and I'll be on hand if either of you fail so that I can finish the job," she announced.

I grinned at that; she had totally grown on me.

With that, Kailani used the handcuffs from her guard uniform to cuff my wrists in front of me. I hung my head forward and she and Raife marched me out of the fenced-in area and over to the main road. The streets were sparsely populated now; everyone had run into their homes seemingly due to the commotion at the front gates.

We walked down a few more roads and then hung a right. I flicked my gaze up to see a giant palace with large columns in front of it. It loomed up ahead and my stomach tied into knots. There were over two dozen guards, fully armed, standing beside each column. The wind rushed past us and I wondered if it was due to Madelynn and Axil fighting out front.

By the time we reached the first guard at the palace steps, I was a ball of nerves. This was a lot of people to try and control if things went badly. He saw us approaching and broke his formation to meet us before we could get any closer.

"Are you new? Prisoners don't get held here unless we are told to do so by the queen herself," the man said to Raife. "You need to go to the lock-up on Spring Street."

Raife reached out and grasped the sides of my jaw, forcing me to look up at the guard. "Are you dumb? This is the queen of Fallenmoore. We just captured her trying to infiltrate the west wall."

I built up a deep wolfy growl in my throat to add proof to his claim and the soldier paled as he looked down at my cuffed hands. Reaching behind him, he pulled out a separate pair of cuffs and then yanked me from Kailani's grasp. The second set of cuffs closed around my skin and I knew the moment they touched me that something was wrong. My wolf suddenly felt... very far away.

"You don't use human cuffs on a magic user," he hissed at both Kailani and Raife. With a key, he unlocked the older set of cuffs so that only the newer ones remained.

Human cuffs. That meant ... these newer ones were made for magic users?

I pulled on my wolf, just a little bit, to see if I could get her to come to the surface.

Nothing.

Full-blown panic rose up inside of me and I tried to use the king's power, forcing the man before me to take them off.

Nothing.

"No!" I whimpered and yanked at my wrists, looking up at Kailani with alarm.

I could see her fear just below the surface but she was hiding it, playing her part.

"My bad. Should we drop her off with the lead guard in the dungeon?" Kailani asked.

The man before us had short cropped blond hair and he looked Kailani up and down. "Can you handle that?" he questioned her, since clearly she'd messed up my cuffs.

In one swift move Kailani kicked my knee out and I fell to the ground with a shout. Raife then hooked under my armpit on my left side and Kailani on my right so that they were dragging me. "I can handle it." She blew the guard a kiss and he grinned.

I let my legs go limp, dragging behind me as Raife and Kailani pulled me across the front castle steps.

We passed over two dozen guards and I prayed no one would recognize the elf king's magnificent golden bow strapped to his back. Other guards had bows but they were black with chunky steel.

It felt like it took us forever to reach the front doors of the castle and walk inside. When we stepped into the open entryway it was even busier than outside. Warriors rushed about shouting directions and asking for help at the front wall.

Madelynn and Axil were giving them Hades.

It made me grin.

Kailani herded us down a hallway and then we were alone, suddenly descending a stone staircase.

"I'm so sorry, Zara, did I hurt your knee? I panicked," Kailani whispered as she helped me stand properly so I could walk.

I shook my head. "You did great. I'm not hurt and if I was, I heal fast so don't worry about it." It was true, she'd gotten us all inside which was a miracle.

"Was the flirting necessary?" Raife asked and I sensed his jealousy, which caused me to smile slightly.

"Yes, I think it was. I got us inside, didn't I?" she snapped back.

We reached the bottom steps and the damp smell of a musty dungeon reached my nostrils. Plus one other thing.

Oslo.

His scent was faint, but it was here.

"My brother," I whimpered.

Kailani grasped my upper arm tightly and then looked at her husband. "Get your revenge, my love. I'll help Zara and meet you outside the wall."

Raife looked shocked then, like he hadn't actually believed this day would come. He was here, inside the private castle of the Nightfall queen herself.

He nodded, leaning in to kiss her. "I love you," he whispered and then he disappeared back up the steps.

Kailani stood still, yanking on my cuffs and grunting in desperation. "I don't really know what these are or how they work. I can't get them off," she said.

"I don't care. Take me to my brother. He's scared, I can smell it," I urged her.

With that we walked into the open hallway and then into a larger room surrounded by cells in a circular shape.

At first glance, they all appeared full. When my gaze landed on my brother, head hung low as he hugged his knees, I screamed.

"Oslo!" I ran for him but Kailani hauled me backwards, hard. The two guards who stood in the center of the circular room looked up then.

250

"Who's this?" one of them asked, pulling his knife from his belt.

"Zara Swiftwater, wolven queen." Kailani told them with pride.

He stepped over to me and looked down at my wrists, seemingly to check my cuffs. Then he glanced over at Oslo's cell. "Is that fella who just came in her son?"

Kailani shrugged. "How should I know? I just found her breeching the wall. Queen wants her locked up down here, I assume."

My son. Did I look that old?

"You assumed correct." A powerful female voice entered the room and Kailani went pale, like she'd seen a ghost.

I felt my own inner fear ramp up a notch as the Night-fall queen herself walked into the room. I didn't need to know what she looked like to know who she was. She oozed power. Covered head to toe in red leather, she walked like an alpha, chin tipped high as she held our gaze.

"Cuff her. She's not a guard and she's *very* powerful," the queen ordered the guard as she watched Kailani.

The guard scrambled to get the cuffs off his belt and that's when Kailani went berserk. She rushed towards the queen, puckering her lips and sucking the air from the room. I didn't understand what was happening, maybe this was her power? But either way I was going to rush the queen with her. Both of us could definitely take her to the ground. Even as a human with my hands tied behind my back, I was still a powerful fighter.

One second I was turning in Zaphira's direction and the next a funnel of wind picked me up and threw me against the far wall. Oslo screamed as I cracked my head on the stone, slinking to the ground in confusion.

The queen held her hands out, a wind funnel filling the room as she laughed madly. She had fae power? Kailani was on the floor beside me and the guard was affixing the cuffs to her hands. It all happened so fast I barely understood what Zaphira had just done. She had thrown a wind bomb at us.

The Nightfall queen smiled. "You know I realized it wasn't that I wanted to expunge the realm of all magic users," she said and then it started to snow inside the room. She was displaying her variety of powers and I felt sick knowing she'd stolen this from good people. "I just wanted to be one," she added and then a blinding flash of light pulsed in the room, causing my eyes to squint shut.

Footsteps neared and then I smelled her right beside me but my vision was black. She'd blinded me, hopefully temporarily. "But there is one gift I have been waiting to acquire," she whispered in my ear then stroked my cheek, pressing her warm fingers against the side of my face. "A powerful alpha wolf."

I snapped my head to the right and took in as many fingers as I could into my mouth, then I bit down.

Hard.

Warm coppery blood gushed over my tongue as my canines severed one of her fingers and then the queen's blood-curdling scream rang throughout the room.

I spat the finger onto the ground, laughing manically in the hopes that she would fear I was mentally unstable. Cyrus would approve.

"My finger!" she bellowed in a guttural scream. "Get me a healer."

Shapes started to dance before my eyes as my vision slowly returned, and I prepared myself for her retaliation. Some dark shape sailed towards me and before I could decipher what it was, there was a crack to the side of my head and once again, blackness overtook me.

"Zara." Oslo's sweet voice pulled me from my unconscious state and I opened my eyes, blinking rapidly. My vision had returned but a deep headache throbbed at the base of my skull.

My little brother peered down at me in fear. "There's blood coming out of your head."

Kailani swam into view then, looking worse for wear. Her hair was messed up, like someone had tried to rip it out, and her lip was split.

She probed the back of my skull with her fingers and I hissed. "It's stopped bleeding," she told Oslo. "She'll be okay. Your kind naturally heal. No need for healers most of the time."

He nodded, seeming more assured.

Then she looked down at me, grinning like a fool.

I peered around us to take in our surroundings. Maybe there was a reason for her gleefulness. Nope. We were locked up inside a cell. People from the other neighboring cells stared over at us with curiosity.

"What could you possibly be happy about?" I asked her.

She tried to control her smile but when she pulled it back down, it just popped right back up. "You bit her finger off!" she finally blurted and then burst into laughter. "Are you insane? I mean it was amazing. You should have seen her. 'My finger! My finger! Find it!'" Kailani mimicked and now I was grinning too.

I looked over at Oslo and he too had a slight lift to his lips.

"You got her good," he said.

I sat up slowly, assessing the damage. Other than the head injury, everything else seemed to be in working order.

"But, Zara, you made her mad. She could have killed you," Oslo added.

I shook my head. "She showed her hand. She wants my power. She won't kill me until she has that."

Kailani nodded. "Your sister is right. She wants both of our powers: she won't kill us."

"Zara," Oslo's voice cracked. "I have to tell you something."

I couldn't do this right now. Not with him. "I know," I said and reached out to smooth his hair. "And we can't think about it right now because we have to stay strong, okay? Cyrus would want that."

Oslo's eyes filled with tears at the mention of our big brother's name but he nodded. I would fall to pieces later, both Oslo and I would, and Axil would help put us together, but right now I couldn't think about anything but getting my brother to safety.

"Psst," someone from the cell next to ours pulled our attention.

I looked up to see a lithe-looking female fae with long blonde hair, pointed ears and dirt-crusted nails. She seemed like she'd been here for a while.

She motioned that I come closer and so I stood, waiting a second for the dizziness to abate and then approached her.

Kailani stepped over to her as well and when we were only a few inches from her face she pointed to the metal bars between us. "When they first pulled me and my little sister in here, they didn't have any more of the magic suppression cuffs like you have on." She indicated to our hands that were bound in front of us.

I nodded but was wondering where she was going with this. She looked around at the center of the room where two guards were chatting happily and not paying attention to us.

"I was able to use my dragon-folk fire magic and winter fae ice magic to snap one of the bars off here." She pointed between us and I looked down as she pulled the bar away to reveal a decent-sized gap. She then quickly replaced it in case a guard was looking. Now that I peered closer it was simply wedged between the top and bottom supports but not attached.

"And I did another at the window." She tipped her head to the opening at the upper end of her cell, her cuffed hands hanging in front of her. "My little sister is the same size as your brother. She got free and they haven't noticed."

My breath hitched as I realized what she was saying. The gap wasn't large enough for a full-grown man or woman, but a small child could fit through with some help.

"You're half dragon, half fae?" Kailani asked her.

The woman nodded and that explained it. Fire and ice. Fire and ice enough times throughout the night and it would snap metal like the blacksmiths did.

"Thank you." A lump formed in my throat as I was overcome with emotion.

"Your sister was in this cell?" Kailani asked.

The woman bobbed her head. "We did it at night when the guard was asleep but I fear you don't have that long if the Nightfall queen wants your magic. They will torture him to get you to agree."

She was right. And very smart.

"What do you suggest?" I asked her. She'd clearly been here longer than me and was quick-thinking.

She eyed the cell behind her. "I'll ask the people locked up across the room to create a diversion in ten minutes' time. The guards will rush to that side, and then your brother makes his move."

I nodded, reaching for her fingers through the bars and grasping them. She had no idea what a gift this was. To not have to worry about Oslo being tortured if I didn't comply with whatever the queen would want.

"Thank you," I said again.

She gave me a weak smile. "We need to stick together."

With that she turned away from me and went across her cell to speak to the fae man neighboring her. She whispered something to him and he nodded, walking across the length of his cell and passing a message to the next person. I could see now that this message would get all the way to the other side of the room and in ten minutes' time, we would have our distraction.

Now I needed to prepare my soft-hearted little brother to break out of here and find his way to safety. *Alone.*

Walking over to Oslo, I watched him as he glanced at me with fear-filled eyes. I was always so easy on him, coddling him and snuggling him. I couldn't do that anymore, I needed him to be strong for this.

Placing my cuffed hands on one side of his shoulder, I

met his eyes and I saw so much of our beautiful mother in them.

I kept my voice low. "In ten minutes, there will be a distraction across the room that will take up the guards' attention. Then we will open a space small enough between the bars for you to wiggle out of our cell and into the next—" He started to protest but I shut him down with a glare. "Then our new friend will hoist you up to her window where another bar will be removed and you will slip out of the window and into the outside. From there you will run to the storm drain at the east wall. It's a metal cap in the ground near the community garden. Go inside, it goes under the wall and exits the city."

"You're coming right?" he asked with so much innocence it tore at my heart.

I shook my head. "I'm too big. But you're twelve now. You need to start toughening up."

His bottom lip quivered and I wanted to pull him to my chest and hold him but I kept us an arm's length apart. "When you get out of the storm drain on the other side of the gates, I want you to shift into wolf form. Avoid the big areas of fighting. Make your way south-west to Thorngate but go farther if you have to in order to avoid the war, you can always circle back. Tell the fae king you are my brother and he will protect you."

His chest heaved as he held my gaze and it was the first time he'd stared at me for so long. It was the one glimmer of hope I had that he might be strong enough to endure this.

"You're a small wolf, you can hide in bushes and—" my voice broke as I swallowed a sob. I'd just remembered that Cyrus was dead and this was the only family I had left other than Axil and our unborn child.

I shook him a little. "I love you too damn much, Oz! You have to be strong for me and do this, okay?"

He growled then. A low and firm growl of dominance. "I can do this," he assured me and then I did pull him to my chest. I crushed that kid against me and breathed him in as if it were the last time I might ever see him. Because it might be.

"You're gonna get out too though, right? Eventually?" he mumbled against my ear.

I pulled back and gave him a knowing look. "This is me we're talking about," I said confidently, though I felt anything but. I noticed he wasn't wearing cuffs. They probably weren't worried about a scrawny kid shifting into a wolf and harming anyone. But I was cuffed, and that meant I was about as useless as a human. But I wouldn't tell him that.

A commotion started at the far end of the room, shouting and fighting, and the guards immediately moved that way.

This was it.

"I love you, Oslo. You're such a good kid. Mom and

dad would be so proud." I tried to stay strong but tears leaked down my cheeks.

"I love you too, Zar," he said and wiped at his own cheeks.

Damn. I prayed to the Maker then, which I hardly did, and asked that my little brother be protected.

"Psst," the woman called to us and I knew we were on limited time. Kailani positioned her body to face the skirmish at the far end of the room but against the bars so that she could block what we were about to do. The fae-dragon hybrid woman removed the bar easily and Oslo looked at me one last time. I gave him an encouraging smile and he turned his body sideways, slipping through the bars. He got halfway when his ear got stuck and he hissed. I gave him a hard shove and he popped out into the other cell. The bar was replaced quickly and then the woman shuffled him across the room and I spun to watch the guards break up the fight, both of their attention fully engaged.

My heart hammered in my chest as I peered back to see the woman had already boosted my brother up to the window and he pulled the middle bar off, shimmying his arms through to the other side. All I could do was pray that there was no one out patrolling on the other side of that wall. We were halfway submerged underground so when he did get out, if he could stay low, he might be able to get away unseen. He'd look human to any passerby in Nightfall City so I just had to hope for the best or the worry would drive me insane.

I steeled myself as one of the guards left the cell in which the fight had been broken up and made his way to the center of the room.

Glancing over my shoulder, I noticed that the woman was still halfway through shoving my brother out the window. It was an extremely tight fit and he was having to crawl on his elbows to pull himself through.

I scrambled for ideas on how to get the guard to look away but my mind was drawing a blank. Anything I did would just draw his attention in this direction.

"Hey!" a male in one of the cells to the left side of the room shouted. The guard turned in his direction and then the man pulled his trousers down and flashed his backside, pressing it against the bars. "Kiss my arse, you bloodsucker sell-outs!" he cried.

The guard pulled out a baton and ran forward, rapping it hard against the bars and the man fell forward laughing.

"That's enough!" the guard yelled. "Or you'll all be put down!"

I looked back at the window just in time to see the woman replace the bar with shaking cuffed hands and then face forward as if nothing happened. I could just see Oslo's feet as they grew smaller in the distance and he ran away.

Tears built up in my eyes but I forced them down.

He was safe. Now it was time to fight.

I walked closer to the bars and pressed my face against

them, looking at the man who had helped distract the guard.

I gave him a nod which I hoped conveyed my gratitude. He nodded back in solidarity.

Kailani stood next to me then, laying her head on my shoulder. It was the equivalent of a hug. Or the best you could do for a hug when you were both handcuffed.

"Do you have family?" I asked her.

"Just my aunt. No siblings. Parents are dead," she replied matter-of-factly.

"Mine too. He ... was, is all I have," I told her.

She nudged me and forced me to face her. There was a calmness in her gaze that brought me peace.

"We're going to get out of this and then you, Madelynn, Arwen and I are going to go on a yearly women's retreat. Like the men did when they were younger," she declared.

I grinned. "Oh yeah?"

She nodded. "There is an elvin spa I know of that gives great massages and they have mud baths and all the confections you could hope to eat."

"What will the men do without us?" I inquired, playing into her fantasy because it was taking my mind off things.

"Watch the children and tend to the kitchen of course," she replied which caused me to bark out into laughter.

My face fell pretty quickly though. "How did we get here? War. It seems so ... wrong."

She looked at the guards. "Hatred. Division. If people focused on what they had in common, or how they could help one another, rather than how they were different, it would solve a lot of problems."

Well said.

"Kailani?"

She looked at me seriously.

"Zaphira killed my big brother. She kidnapped my little brother. I can't let her live. I may have to lose my life in order to kill her, so please tell Axil I'm sorry."

Her face fell at that and she looked at my stomach where a child grew inside of me. I didn't want to think about that right now. I just wanted revenge. It was a steady banging war drum in my chest, a thirst that could not be quenched until Zaphira's head was severed from her body.

Kailani nodded. "You will have a small window of time if they put you in the machine that steals your magic. They take off your cuffs. Only then can you use your power to try and overtake them."

I dipped my chin in understanding. "Thank you."

We fell silent then, sitting against the bars and waiting for the next move. Eventually someone would come take one or both of us. And after several hours, they did. My head had fully healed by the time the guard came for Kailani and me.

"Where are you taking us?" Kailani asked as we were hauled out of the cell.

"Shut up," the guard told her and then peered into the cell, blinking rapidly. "Where is the kid?"

"Do you want me to answer or should I shut up?" Kailani said.

He reached up and smacked her hard across the face and her lip split back open.

"They already took him!" I screamed at him.

He glared at me. "Where? Who?"

Kailani was holding her cheek. "How should we know? We don't work here. A guard took him to the lab."

He growled and pointed the sharp tip of a knife at my throat. "Walk and don't get any ideas or I start stabbing."

I did as he asked, feeling like it was a good sign that my brother hadn't been brought back down to the dungeon since he'd left.

Was he free? Already outside the gates? Was Axil okay? I felt for our bond, hidden among all of my anxiety for my brother, and could sense that he was still alive. I would know if my mate was dead, right?

We were marched up the stairs and down a hallway to a large dining room. Outside the room, two more guards were stationed. One of them broke away and stepped up beside Kailani. "They're ready," he said to the guard that held us.

They?

The doors opened and I steeled myself as I took in the

space before us. The Nightfall queen sat at the head of a large table with a regal-looking bloodsucker next to her. I didn't know anything about necromerian royalty but this man reeked of power and influence. His black high-collared jacket framed his pale face and he stared at me with a gaze I didn't like. One that was hungry, like a half-starved animal.

They both watched us as we entered and the queen gave me a snarl. I glanced at her bandaged hand and grinned.

"You can have her wolf power, Regis, but I want the elf queen," she told him.

Regis looked at me and squinted. "She's the wife of Axil Moon?" he asked and my stomach tightened. They knew his name.

"I believe they call them mates, but yes," Zaphira replied.

We were led to the table where two places had been set across from the queen and her companion. Kailani and I shared a look.

What was the game plan here? Feed us dinner and then steal our magic? Why? To play with us?

Just when I was beginning to wonder if we were meant to take a seat or not, the guard pushed me down into one of the chairs. I was seated across from the man Zaphira had called Regis, who I was going to assume was the necros' king.

"What will you be having for dinner? Blood with a side of blood?" I asked him sarcastically.

He shared a look with the queen and she nodded. "See. She has a temper: those make for the best magic elixirs."

I swallowed hard at that. If Kailani was right, I'd have only seconds from when they took off my cuffs to when they placed me in the machine. And if I couldn't fight back, I remembered my promise to Raife and I would not falter. There was no way I was giving her this power. I'd carve my own heart out before that happened.

A waiter brought out three plates of food, setting them before the queen, Kailani and me. Then he set a glass of dark red fluid in front of the king.

Regis looked at the waiter in disgust. "I prefer it straight from the source." Then he turned to the queen. "May I?" he asked, his eyes on me.

Zaphira nodded and I stiffened. "Oh, please do."

Kailani squirmed in her seat beside me. "Won't that affect the power transfer?" she asked nervously and I could tell she was stalling for time.

"No," the queen said and then before I could even track his movements, the king was beside me, my face in his hands. I moved to fight back and then his mouth was on my neck. A small pinch bit at my skin and then a wave of nausea rolled over me as he sucked.

"Stop this!" Kailani shouted, jerking beside me, but the

guard held her firmly in place. The slurping sounds at my neck were making me want to vomit but not as much as the slight buzz of pleasure that hummed just under my skin. He had some kind of magic spell over me that was making me think I liked it. With one jerk of my head I cracked my skull into his and he pulled away from me laughing.

The moment his mouth released my neck, the pleasure faded and was replaced by a dull throb.

Zaphira took a bite of her meat, grinning. "Does she taste good?"

Regis stood. "Oh, you have no idea. And not just that, she is linked to her mate. I could feel him, far away but there."

I froze, swallowing hard. He *felt* the pack bonds? I calmed myself and searched for Axil. I could feel him alive and anxious but there. Had the necro king felt that too? That wasn't right, but then I had no idea what kind of power necros held.

Regis walked over to the queen's plate of food and grasped her meat knife. "I wonder ... Do you think her mate can feel it if I hurt her?"

Kailani and I both bucked in our seats at that but the guards kept us firmly in place. My heart crashed wildly in my chest but I was helpless to stop him.

The queen nodded and then held out her bandaged hand, showcasing her missing finger which was now a bloody stump hidden under white gauze. "I require revenge, my love."

My love?

One second he stood beside her and then next my hand was being pulled out onto the dinner table, fingers splayed out.

"No!" Kailani screamed, thrashing her back against her chair.

The necromerian king held the blade to my pinky finger and I went eerily still, resigning myself to my fate. Cyrus taught me that wounds hurt more when you resisted them.

Control where they hurt you.

I curled my other fingers into a ball and willingly gave him my pinky, looking at Kailani to let her know it was okay. Tears streamed down her face and then ... the dining hall doors burst open and a young man stumbled in, grasping his throat. His face was purple, and white foam bubbled at his lips. Regis and Zaphira both froze.

"Who is that?" Regis asked, perplexed.

Zaphira's fork clattered onto the plate and her hand shook. "My food taster."

She smacked her lips together and then reached up to grab her throat in anticipation. Staring at Kailani, she leapt into a standing position. "You can save me! Regis, she can save me!"

The queen was coughing now, clearing her throat uncontrollably. She stumbled forward, falling onto the table as she gasped for breath and rolled onto her back, looking up at the ceiling.

The necromerian king went from being about to cut my finger off to zooming over to Kailani and pressing the blade to her throat. He was so fast it was unnerving. A worthy adversary had this been a fair fight.

"Save her," he commanded and then looked at the guards. "Uncuff her!"

The queen's lips were purple now, white spittle forming on them as she rasped for breath.

Kailani stood, looked down at Zaphira and smiled. "I would rather die than save her. So kill me now and be done with it."

Pure pride flooded through me at that. Kailani *was* an alpha: she had no fear of death.

Regis snarled, moving to do just that when I burst from where I sat, cracking the guard behind me over the head. As I did so, the whistle of arrows tore through the room and then the sickening thunks of the tips embedding into flesh.

I blinked and then backed up as the necromerian king fell backwards, three arrows in his chest and one in the side of his head.

Two more thuds and then each guard went down, an arrow right in each of their hearts.

The curtains moved at the far wall and then Raife stood before us, bow drawn.

"You okay, ladies?" he asked us, but kept his eyes on the gasping queen. She was barely breathing, her body twitching and seizing before us as she clawed at her purple face.

We both nodded and I reached down and grabbed a tiny ornate key the guard had hanging from his waist belt. I used it to free Kailani and then she was able to unlock mine.

Leaning forward, Raife held the tip of his arrow to the queen's throat. She had acquired all these powers and yet was too weak to use even one against him.

"This is for my family," he said and watched as she twitched and gasped for breath, suffering greatly.

Her eyes bulged wider.

"And my brother," I added.

Kailani got close to her, leaning into her ear. "And every other person harmed by your existence."

One last twitch and then she went still, lips crusted white, face purple and eyes bulging. It was a horrific sight and yet I didn't feel satisfied. Grasping the steak knife, I rammed it into her chest, right where her heart was. "Just in case," I told the room.

Raife dropped his arrow tip to the ground and fell back against the wall. He sighed, looking relieved. For years he'd chased that revenge. I had no idea what it had done to him but it would have eaten me alive. Knowing I would go home to Cyrus' dead body killed me but this brought me at least some measure of comfort.

"Not to ruin the moment but in times of war, if we take her head to her lead general, he has to call a cease fire.

People are probably dying on the front lines so ..." Kailani glanced at her husband.

Raife nodded, pulling the sword from his hip and Kailani looked away as he took the queen's head clean off. Knotting his fingers into her hair, he exited the dining hall with me and his wife beside him. Now that I was no longer cuffed, I pulled the power I had borrowed from Axil to the surface.

If anyone tried anything, I would make them kneel.

Raising her head into the air, Raife gave a battle cry and walked out the front doors of the Nightfall castle.

The warriors perched on the front steps looked up at him startled and when they saw the head of their leader they gasped in shock.

They pulled out their weapons, but I used my power to blanket them with a command to freeze.

"The war is over!" Kailani bellowed. "Your queen is dead and as such you must surrender and open the gates!"

I relaxed my power over the two dozen men and one of them stepped forward and turned to another and nodded. "Get General Ibsen."

The guard took off and then we waited as another guard ran to the front gates. Everyone seemed confused as to what they should do. Their leader was dead, I had the power to control them, and the war between our peoples was over.

A moment later the front gates of Nightfall City opened and dozens of wolves ran inside. I grinned when I noticed the Royal Wolven Guard with Lucien leading them. It looked like they had been able to win on the front lines then make their approach all the way to the castle. People backed up in fear and guards dropped their weapons. I scanned the people flooding into the city. Among them was Madelynn, and—

The moment I saw Axil in human form, with my little brother holding his hand and walking next to him, I started running.

"Axil! Oslo!" I called to them, my feet pounding the ground as I closed the distance between us. My little brother broke away from Axil first and ran to greet me, crashing into me with a big hug. He was covered in dirt and twigs but otherwise seemed unharmed. Axil was next. Pulling me into his arms with Oslo squashed between us, he captured my mouth in a kiss and then placed his hand on my belly. "You're okay?" he asked.

I nodded.

I was now. The queen was dead and my little surviving family was safe and secure.

20

It was a bit chaotic over the next hour. I'd sent Oslo back to Lucien's castle with some trusted guards to remain with Arwen's twins until this was over. Soldiers watched wearily as the kings and queens of Avalier amassed in the front of their castle steps. They were disarmed by our wolves and asked to wait off to the side. Their queen's head was displayed on a spike in the center of town for all to see. The war was over, and we would not tolerate any uprising. Arwen and Drae had just arrived and now we were all assembled.

General Ibsen had surrendered and left to fetch

Queen Zaphira's eldest heir. Apparently, she kept them spread apart within her realm.

We'd blown the horn of surrender and the fighting at the borders had ceased as well.

We released the prisoners from the dungeon and every Nightfall citizen was told to wait in their homes. A curfew was in effect and we wanted as few people on the streets as possible in case there was a skirmish with the new Nightfall king.

We were about to tell Zaphira's son that we'd killed his mother and the war with our people was over. If he didn't pledge an alliance with us, we'd kill him too. She had six more living sons if I'd heard Drae right. So we'd kill each one until one of them signed a peace treaty with our kind and stopped the fighting.

The moments ticked by and then finally two men rode through the open gates, each atop a horse.

One was General Ibsen and the other was a man whom I assumed to be the new king of Nightfall. As he neared, I took him in. He sat tall and was muscular. More than the elves, less than the wolven. His dark wavy hair fell in a stylish quiff to his sharp chin and his eyes were dark hazel. I was pleased to see that they held a kindness that his mother's had lacked. It was hard to deny how handsome he was.

He stepped down off his horse and stood before all eight of us. He wore metallic battle armor with the Nightfall crest; it was clean and looked unused. It was clear he hadn't been on the battlefield lately and was probably only wearing it as a formality. He glanced once at his mother's head on the spike but I saw no emotion there. Either he was good at hiding it, or he simply didn't care that she'd died.

Bowing his head deeply with respect, he met our gazes. "I am Prince Callen. I am told that my mother has been killed and we have surrendered in the war."

He was all business and tough exterior, showing no emotion, which I respected.

Drae stepped forward: we had agreed he would speak on our behalf. "You are *King* Callen now. If you want it. We only require that you sign a one-hundred-year peace treaty to never start war with our realms again."

Callen seemed to consider Drae's words, peering around at his mother's loyal warriors who stood on the outskirts of our conversation. "And if I *don't* sign it?" he asked.

Okay, that wasn't a good sign.

"Then we kill you and move to the next heir in your line of succession until one agrees."

Callen looked like he'd expected that. "Right then, shall we take this negotiation inside?" he asked with a flick of his eyebrows.

There was something in his face. Something that said he had more to say but didn't want to speak in front of his mother's warriors.

Drae inclined his head. "It's not a negotiation, but sure."

With that, Axil and I led the way into the castle which had been cleared of his people and was now crawling with ours. A wolven warrior stood at the opening of every hall and doorway.

When Callen entered the castle, he moved to go to the dining room but I pulled out a hand to stop him.

"You're not going to want to see what's in there."

Your mother's headless body, I wanted to say.

Dawning realization played out on his face and he moved away from that door and to another. We stepped inside and found ourselves in a large study with a sparse desk and one chair behind it.

Callen moved behind the desk and sat in the chair as we all fanned out around it. Kailani closed the door.

Once we were in the private space, Callen let out a long sigh. "I apologize for my apparent reluctance to sign this treaty. I had to play coy for my mother's loyalists."

Drae nodded. "So you'll sign the treaty?"

Callen brushed his fingers through his hair. "Of course. But I might not live through the night if I do. My mother was an extremist, she and I didn't agree on anything. Her men are loyal to her ideals." His hands shook a little and my heart softened. He was genuinely fearful for his life, that much was clear.

"Do you have your own army?" Drae asked him.

He reached up to rub his temples. "I would hardly call

them an army. I have twenty loyal men at a fort about one hour's ride east of here."

Drae shared a look with Lucien who dipped his head in agreement. Lucien glanced at Axil and Raife, and then it was as if they all shared some unspoken understanding.

Drae cleared his throat. "Sign the treaty now and we will keep three hundred of our men posted here until you can transition over to new leadership. You'll have to weed out who is loyal to your mother's ideals and who would best serve you."

Callen stilled, his mouth opening in shock. "You would do that?"

"We want this to be a lasting peace and will invest whatever it takes to do that," Raife added.

It was a great idea and would be more lasting if he could dispose of his mother's loyalists.

Callen looked over at the elf king and swallowed hard. "I'm ... sorry for what my mother has done to your families and your people."

An apology? I hadn't expected that. These types of takeovers were usually fraught with tension.

"Were you close with her?" I asked, trying to gauge how this normal and seemingly kind human came from her.

He barked out a laugh. "She wasn't capable of closeness. Or love. No, me and my brothers each stayed with her until we were seven. Then we were sent away to live elsewhere and raised by a nanny. None of us share a father. She just wanted heirs to continue her bloodline. My eldest brother was the only one she was close with and he's dead."

My heart tightened then. Only with his mother until seven and then on his own? It was horrible and I thought of Oslo in that moment and how young and sweet he was at seven. He'd needed so much love and reassurance then.

"Will your other brothers try to take over?" Raife asked. I could sense the concern in his voice now too.

Callen let out a shaky breath. "I ... honestly don't know. We aren't close. She kept us apart. I doubt anyone wants the responsibility. We all have our own lands to manage and are all independently wealthy. We have no desire to rule a kingdom."

The burden of one's lineage was something I knew Axil could relate to and in that moment he slipped his hand into mine.

"Are you married? Children?" Drae asked him.

He shook his head. "I run a profitable ore mine, no time for a wife."

Arwen chuckled at that. "Well, you're king now, that means taking a wife and having children."

We'd suddenly all taken to giving this young man counsel on how to rule.

He looked stunned then. "I guess so."

He appeared so overwhelmed and I felt for him, but we needed to make sure that this was a smooth transition so that Nightfall never rose to power again.

"I have an idea," I proposed and everyone looked at me. "King Callen, this is your chance to change things, make them better than they were before," I told him and he nodded his head in agreement. "What if, along with signing the peace treaty, you agreed to take a wife from one of our realms?"

The entire room fell into a stunned silence. His mother had been a purist, humans against those of us with magic. And then when she couldn't naturally have what we had, she stole it.

"It would send a message to your people that the new Nightfall kingdom is one of inclusion. Not just an empty peace treaty with our kind, but one married into with generations of heirs," Drae added, seemingly delighted with my idea.

Callen swallowed hard, as if the very idea of marrying a woman who shifted into an animal terrified him. "Please forgive my ignorance, as I live on a mountain and do not travel often. Could I ... have healthy children with someone who is not my kind?"

Kailani chuckled at that. "Of course! Your children will be half human, half whatever your wife is. They would have some of her abilities, whatever those might be. I'm half elf."

He relaxed after hearing that and I had to remind myself that this man had been sheltered away in the mountains and probably fed lies about our people his entire life.

"It was just a suggestion," Drae said. "But it might be too much of a leap from—"

"No, I think it's a good idea. A marriage to bridge our kingdoms. I would be honored to choose a wife from any of your realms," he said diplomatically but I could hear the nerves in his voice. I wondered if it was because he'd just agreed to choose a wife who carried magic, or that he'd have to get married at all. He was very handsome and young and had just admitted he was rich. I was betting he could have any woman he wanted where he lived. He'd have to give that up, become king and change his entire life overnight. It was a lot to process.

Drae pulled the prewritten treaty out and spread it across his desk. "Alright, well if you sign here, we can announce your desire to take a wife while our men are still posted here just in case there is backlash."

He grasped his quill and ink. "I appreciate that," he told Drae. "I can't imagine that news will be taken well."

"You might be surprised," Kailani offered. "I grew up here and many of the people just did what your mother said because they were scared of her, not because they agreed."

Drae held out a hand over the treaty, blocking Callen from signing. "Don't you want to read it first?" he asked. "It also requires the destruction of all of your mother's magic-stealing machines."

Callen shivered. "I hated that invention. Good riddance. I just want peace upon our lands."

Drae moved his hand and Callen signed easily as each one of us sighed in relief.

It was done and by my account it looked like Callen was already shaping up to be a decent king.

One by one we shook his hand and I had to admit he'd earned my respect. It would be hard for him from here on out but he seemed up to the task with a little help.

"And I hate to add another thing but your mother had aligned with the necromerians and we killed their king too. He's in your dining room." I winced as I told him.

His eyes bugged. "The necros?"

So I was right, he hadn't been on the battlefield. The outfit was all for show.

"There might be retaliation for that. You will want to amass a council to give you advice," Lucien offered.

"I need a drink," Callen said and we all burst into laughter.

Drae reached across the desk and clapped Callen on the shoulder. "It will be okay, young king. Just pretend you have it all figured out, until you really do."

"Noted," Callen offered, but was wearing a rueful smile.

With that, we left. The war that I hadn't even known about two weeks ago was over and now all that was left to do was bury our dead and mend our hearts.

21

I was actually showing a little, my belly slightly swollen with pregnancy. It had been two months since the war ended and we'd decided to get together in Archmere with all the kings and queens of Avalier to have a memorial ceremony for our fallen ones. I'd buried my brother Cyrus the day we'd gotten back and then promptly fallen into a week-long depression. The only things that pulled me out of it was Oslo, Axil and this baby.

I rubbed my belly, sucking on the piece of ginger my lady-in-waiting had cut for me this morning to keep the nausea down. Eliza sat next to me in the carriage as Oslo rode alongside Axil. Axil was teaching Oslo all of the manly things one needed to know to be an alpha and leader. Since Oslo's escape from the dungeon in Nightfall, he had shown great dominance and seemed to be coming into his own.

Axil said in another three years he would give Oslo a safe position in his army to start learning the ropes and one day my brother would make a good commander.

"Auntie 'Liza," Eliza said, pulling my attention from my thoughts.

"What?"

"I'm trying on names for the baby to call me. Eliza is too long."

I smiled at my pack sister. Although Axil had claimed me for Death Mountain pack, and Eliza had remained with Mud Flat, we had a bond that could still be felt as if we were in the same pack. No one could explain it. It was unbreakable. Forged with trust and a life debt on both sides.

"Auntie Liz." I shortened it even more.

Eliza grinned. "I love that."

Eliza had flourished in the Mud Flat pack. She'd not been dominant enough to take my spot but she was sixth, which was still pretty impressive. She lived in my childhood home and helped to take care of my brother's widow and my nephews that he'd left behind. I went out there to visit them once a month.

"Amara told me you've been spending long nights

with Shane under the stars," I said in a syrupy sweet voice. "What's going on there?"

Eliza scoffed. "A lady doesn't kiss and tell."

"So, there's kissing!" I accused.

She burst out laughing, going bright red in the cheeks which made me smile too. Her laugh was contagious and I was so grateful that against all odds, we'd both made it out of the Queen Trials alive.

We slowed, and Axil popped his head in. "We're here."

I wasn't used to riding in a carriage but now that I was a pregnant queen, Axil said a wolf sled wasn't appropriate or safe enough.

We descended from the carriage and Oslo dismounted, slipping his hand into mine.

"Are they going to have Cyrus' name carved into a tree or something?" he asked me.

I reached up and smoothed his stray hairs. "I don't know. Probably not." The elves had asked to be responsible for the task of honoring the fallen. Five hundred and thirty-seven bodies were recovered from the war. Fae, dragon-folk, elvin and wolven. I didn't know what kind of memorial they would do but Kailani had sounded pretty excited about it in her last letter to me.

It was just getting dark, the sun setting on the horizon. The elves had been very clear that the unveiling of the memorial should be at sunset.

Hundreds of people had traveled from throughout the

realm to be here tonight. I spotted Madelynn in the crowd with Lucien and she waved me over. When we reached them, she pulled me in for a hug and squeezed. "You're showing!" she cooed over my belly and I smiled at her. Axil and Lucien clapped each other on the back and then Kailani was suddenly before us.

"Hurry or you'll miss it!" she said and yanked me by the hand, pulling me and Oslo towards the open space they had prepared for the event. It was set at the base of a beautiful mountain and in the center of the meadow was a breathtaking, gigantic, weeping willow tree.

Raife stood before the tree wearing a stylish silver tunic and Kailani pulled me right past all the crowds of people and up to the front. She knew how hard my brother's loss had hit me and I thought it was sweet she had put so much time in this memorial for the fallen ones.

Raife cleared his throat and then pointed to his wife. "I would like to honor my queen, my wife, my love, Kailani. This was her idea and she met with all of the artists and watched over the whole project."

Everyone clapped, me included, as Kailani blushed beside her husband.

"And a big thank you to all of the local artists who made this memorial possible and worked tirelessly." Raife then gestured with his hand and over fifty artists stepped out from the crowd and assembled before us.

We applauded loudly as they bowed, accepting the praise with gratitude. As they moved to the sides, opening up the clearing again, I noticed the weeping willow tree had leaves or flowers or something on it. They were glinting in the dying light as if made of metal.

"The Nightfall war took a lot from us," Raife said, "but we now look forward to a reign of peace that we will try to find solace in." He then gestured to the tree. "May the souls of the fallen ones be with their Maker forever. Please come closer, and when the sun sets, you will see the surprise." The crowd pushed forward then, and I grasped Oslo's hand and moved closer. With every step we took towards the magnificent tree, the metal objects became clearer.

They were metal, but they weren't flowers. They were butterflies! Tiny sculptures hooked onto the tree. The center of the body of each butterfly was formed of beautiful crystal.

I walked right up to one of them and peered at the intricate wing design. There, engraved along the outside of the wing in tiny perfect script, was a phrase.

We honor Thomas Colt.

A lump formed in my throat.

I read another.

We honor Cassady Readers.

Kailani appeared at my side and motioned us to a weeping strand near the base of the tree. There was a little gold butterfly and engraved on the wing was, *we honor Cyrus Swiftwater.*

Oslo took one look at it and began to wipe at his

leaking eyes. I tried but couldn't hold back the tears. Normally I would call them weak and try not to show emotion but my brother was worth every tear I had cried for him.

"It's so beautiful," I told Kailani as she watched my reaction.

Reaching over, she patted my back. "Look." She pointed to the center of the butterfly and I had to rapidly blink to make sure I wasn't seeing things.

The sun had left us and now the crystals in the center of the butterflies were glowing! At first it was barely noticeable but as the sky grew darker, the butterflies all took on a beautiful purple hue.

Gasps rang throughout the space as the tree lit up like the moon. Over five hundred glowing butterflies.

"These crystals never go dark!" Raife yelled. "They are charged by sunlight and will glow, each night, until the end of time! Just as the memories of those fallen ones will always be with us."

A few people burst into sobs and I pulled Oslo into my arms. Suddenly Axil was there holding us both and I knew it was the perfect remembrance for my brother. His light would never fade, just as the memories of him would never leave me.

Epilogue

One Year Later

"As an alpha, you will need to stare death in the face and laugh," Axil told our three-month-old son Koa Cyrus Moon as he lay nestled in his father's arms. Koa looked up at his father with bright blue eyes as spit bubbles formed on his lips and I smiled.

"Teaching him the ways of the big bad wolf?" I asked as I entered the room.

Axil looked up at me with adoration. "Alpha training starts young."

I snickered. "Quite young indeed."

I moved to his side and placed a kiss on his cheek. "You sure you guys will be okay without me for three days?"

"Are you kidding? Koa has two wet nurses, his crazy Aunt Liz, and I have an entire palace staff. We'll be fine. Have fun with your friends."

Kailani had arranged the first of our annual queens' retreats. We were going to stay at a well-known elvin hot spring in the mountains for three days. Just me, Kailani, Madelynn and Arwen.

I smiled at him and one of the nursemaids came in to take Koa for his feed. I thanked her, kissing him goodbye and then looked at Axil. Sometimes I couldn't believe that we'd made it. That I'd met my mate at fifteen and against all odds we now stood before each other as husband and wife.

"So, I've been thinking." Axil reached out and yanked me closer to him so that my body slammed flush up against his. "Koa needs a sister," he breathed along my neck and I burst out laughing.

"Koa is still on the breast! A sister can wait." I pawed at his hand which was creeping up the back of my tunic.

Axil pouted, sticking his bottom lip out. "Isn't that why you have two breasts? You can feed two at a time. Arwen does."

I let loose with a wild carefree laugh and I couldn't help but feel my heart swell. "You want a daughter?" I asked him, suddenly dropping into my bedroom voice and letting my eyes go half lidded.

He swallowed hard, nodding. Reaching out, I stroked a single finger against the waist of his trousers and his eyes shuttered closed. Making love to Axil was something I couldn't get enough of. He knew every inch of my body, everything that pleasured me. "What if we get another son?" I asked, raking my lips along his jaw.

"Then we keep trying until I have a daughter who's as feisty and beautiful as her mother," he panted.

I smiled, pulling back to remove my tunic. "What if that takes a dozen children?"

He looked up at me and grinned. "I can think of nothing better than having a dozen children with you, my love."

Dropping to his knees, he kissed my stomach and heat traveled down from my chest to the sensitive spot between my legs. Anticipation thrummed through me. Since Koa's birth, our lovemaking had been sparse. Up late with feedings and his cries of hunger, it was hard to make time for that sort of thing.

Axil trailed his tongue along the ridge of my trousers and I swallowed hard as he untied them and they dropped to the floor.

"I'll be late for my carriage to Archmere," I huffed.

He looked up at me with yellow eyes. "I don't care."

I grinned at his wolf.

Hello, nice to see you.

I loved when Axil got forceful and dominant in bed. "Well, you better make it worth my while then, Axil Moon," I commanded.

With that he lifted me up and threw me over his shoulder, eliciting a squeal from me as he marched me to our marital bed.

When he threw me back down, I could see his gaze drowning in desire as his eyes raked over me. "That sounds like a challenge." His wolf was back and I grinned as he lowered himself on top of me.

We'd done it. Against all odds we'd found our happily ever after and I had to agree with Axil: it was worth the wait.

I WAS LATE TO MY GIRLS' getaway trip but no one seemed to mind. For the next three days it was going to be massages and clay mud masks and girl time. When I arrived, I was led into the living quarters at the elvin spa that Kailani had arranged for us. When I stepped inside the luxurious drawing room, I noticed the three women standing over a platter of dried fruits and cheeses. Arwen spun to face me, her belly swollen with pregnancy.

My mouth dropped open. "You didn't tell me!" I ran to her and Kailani turned as well, showing off a smaller bump than Arwen.

My eyes grew wider. "Is *everyone* pregnant!" I screamed in excitement as I hugged them both.

"Wanted to surprise you all." Arwen patted her belly. "We think it's twins again."

That would scare me but she seemed to take it in her stride.

"Mine better not be twins," Kailani offered.

Madelynn strode over to where I stood and smiled at me, patting her flat stomach. "I'm not pregnant yet. We want to take a year and travel."

She pulled me in for a hug.

"That's a great idea. Come visit us in Fallenmoore," I told her.

"How's little Koa? Keeping you up often in the night?" Kailani asked.

We sat down and talked for hours then. We spoke about family, our hopes and dreams, annoying things our husbands did. Everything. It was so nice to just relax and speak with other strong women and leaders. These ladies had become fierce allies and loyal friends over the past year. Kailani and Raife had traveled in for Koa's birth in case there were any complications. Arwen and Drae flew over with the twins once a month for play dates with Koa, and Madelynn and I had developed a deep friendship through letters. She had a little sister Oslo's age and we both shared the protective burden of taking care of our families.

"Hey," Madelynn said, sipping her wine. "We should

have our kids do a yearly retreat like our husbands did, make sure everyone stays strong and bonded as our kingdoms grow."

"Yes!" Arwen agreed.

"Totally," Kailani chipped in.

I nodded with a smile but a thought struck me. Should we invite any future heirs of Nightfall? The queen was dead and her more sensible son Callen had taken over and was due to be married soon. But the machines that had been destroyed could be rebuilt. Having all of the children of the realm together each year for a retreat would ensure a lasting peace.

"Yes, and we should extend a standing invitation to the future heirs of Nightfall," I added.

All three women went still, seeming to think it over.

"Yes! I love that," Madelynn said as she popped another piece of fruit into her mouth.

Finally, Kailani nodded her agreement. "Agreed. You're so sensible, Zara."

I laughed and Arwen raised her glass of juice to me. "Zara is right. The future of Avalier depends on all realms getting along. Nightfall included."

"Especially them," Madelynn added, raising her glass.

We all clinked and then Arwen sighed. "Should we invite the heirs of Necromere?"

"Don't get crazy," Madelynn told the dragon queen and that caused us all to erupt into fits of laughter.

We then talked for another hour about the war and

how well things were doing now. When the sun started to go down, Arwen stood with a gleeful smile and ran over to her bag in the corner.

Reaching down, she pulled out a brand-new blue tin box and set it on the coffee table.

"What's that?" Kailani asked.

Arwen grinned. "I thought the boys' little memory box was a cute idea. I think we should all write ourselves letters and then open them in twenty years when our kids are grown."

"Yes!" I shot up from where I sat and grabbed a piece of parchment and an ink quill. The others did the same and we all rushed to separate corners of the room.

I plopped down with the parchment in front of me and began to write.

> Dear Future Lara,
>
> In twenty years, you and Axil will probably have a dozen children and they will all be fighting their way up the pack to the most dominant position. Your life was hard in the early years, losing your parents so young, losing Axil at fifteen, having to raise Oslo like a son when you were barely grown yourself. And then losing Cyrus almost broke you. But I hope you can look back on this and smile, because things can only go up

from here. You're a mother to a beautiful little boy, you're a mate to a man who loves you more than life, and most of all, you're strong. You've learned that no matter what life throws at you, you can do hard things. So on the off chance life does throw you some curveballs in the next twenty years, I just want to say ... don't worry. You got this.

You're the strongest woman I know.
Love,
Z

I LOOKED up from the letter, happy to see my girlfriends smiling as well as they wrote their own, then I scribbled a last line.

Oh, and don't ever forget ... Life is better when it's shared with friends. Cherish them.

SOMETHING THAT HAD BEEN empty inside of me since my parents died was filled in that moment. I had everything I could have ever wanted. I had family, friends, a kingdom, a child. I felt so happy and complete and I knew that no matter what life threw my way, I could get through it.

The End

WHAT'S NEXT FROM LEIA:

If you liked this series you will love book one in a hot new fantasy romance by Leia Stone. If Wednesday Addams went to Hogwarts and found herself in the middle of a love triangle. =)

House of Ash and Bone.

ACKNOWLEDGMENTS

Always a big thank you to my amazing readers! I truly could not do this without you. It still amazes me that I get to be creative and do this for a living and someone actually wants to read what I write. Thank you to my Wolf Pack who is so supportive. To Cat and the entire team at HQ, I am so grateful for this partnership and your editing expertise. And always to my husband and children for sharing me with my art. <3

FOLLOW ME

Amazon:

I have over 50 fantasy books for you to enjoy! Check them out on amazon.

Wolf Pack:

Please join my Leia Stone Wolf Pack on Facebook as I often reveal covers and secret bookish things in there as well as doing giveaways.

Newsletter:

Also sign up for my Newsletter at LeiaStone.com so you don't miss a New Release. I don't spam and you can leave anytime.

Social Media:

FOLLOW ME

Follow me on Instagram and Tik Tok and "Like" my Facebook page.